JAY'S SALVATION
THE WINSTONS SERIES
BOOK THREE
ROWENA DAWN
SCARLET LEAF
2018

I0598758

Jay's Salvation

The Winstons, Volume 3

Rowena Dawn

Published by Scarlet Leaf Publishing House, 2020.

Table of Contents

TO MIRELA, A BELOVED FRIEND

THE WINSTONS FAMILY

REBECCA'S CHILDREN
   Adam (m. Anna)
   Evelyne (deceased)
   Adam's children
   Marjorie (Twin, m. Jonathan) – children: Matt (35; M. Nora, adopted son - Nat), Maggie (29), Jay (29)
   Michael (Twin, m. Amelie) – children: Josh (27), Lily (27)
   Gabriel (m. Emilie) – children: Ariel (33), Alex (33), Becka (20; m. Bryan; twins: Lea and Sean)

CHAPTER ONE

A sickening noise of fists hitting flesh filled the alley. Deep groans of pain echoed in their wake. The woman tiptoed and leaned on the wall. She breathed deeply to quiet the adrenaline running through her veins and flexed her shoulders.

She tilted her head and looked around the corner. Her eyes lay on a group of five men, who pummeled another guy in a frenzy. Her heart cringed, and she bit her lower lip.

The poor man did his best to fight against his attackers, but his efforts were vain. The aggressors outnumbered him, and soon, he fell to the ground. The men huddled over the body, prostrated at their feet on the pavement. They started kicking the man in his ribs and back.

The woman threw her thick honey-coloured hair over her shoulder. She took out a scrunchie from the back pocket of her pants and bound her honey-coloured mane in a ponytail so that she could move freely.

Her right hand lifted the hem of her jacket and grabbed the pistol she had shoved into the waistband earlier. She fished an ID out of her sports coat pocket with the fingers of her left hand.

She breathed and exhaled deeply. Now, she felt ready to face the attackers, so she stepped into the alley and shouted, "Police, freeze, or I shoot."

The woman grimaced and rolled her eyes. To her annoyance, the men didn't even turn toward her. They continued to beat the man curled in a ball at their feet to a pulp.

"All right, then," she mumbled. She raised the arm holding the weapon and fired.

The bullet bit the asphalt right next to the foot of one of the goons. That drew the men's attention. They turned to the shooter angrily and forgot about the bleeding victim lying at their feet. The five men scowled and looked ready to jump on her.

The woman lifted her arched eyebrows and shook her head, warning the men to remain where they were. She waved her police ID and showed them her pistol. The five men exchanged a meaningful look among themselves. They didn't seem to worry that the woman was a police officer, but they cared that she had a gun in her hand, and apparently, she knew to use it. So, they began to file back toward the other corner of the alley, keeping the policewoman in their sight all the time.

The scowls on their faces promised fierce retribution, but then, the policewoman didn't show any outward sign of anxiety. She just stared them down with cold eyes until they turned around the corner. Then, a sardonic smile flourished on the woman's lips. Still, she didn't abandon her stance until the men's steps had vanished, and she heard a loud bang. She assumed that the men had slammed the casino's back door behind them.

The policewoman strode in a hurry to the man still curled in a ball on the pavement. His soft groans filled her ears, and she shook her head. Her mouth became a hard line when her eyes laid on the traces of the savage beating the man had suffered.

The policewoman shoved the ID back into her pocket but kept the pistol ready. She hunched next to the man, and her fingers touched his chin gently. She turned the guy's head with care, not to hurt him more than he was.

He tried to look at the woman but couldn't focus his gaze. His nose and mouth bled freely, and one of his eyes was already shut entirely. The other was swollen and bloody.

'It will be much worse tomorrow,' the woman shook her head with regret. The man's face looked as if he had gone through the wrangler, and her heart cringed again. *'Such a pity,'* she thought. *'You've been such a handsome guy,'* she reflected with bitterness.

Indeed, the policewoman had been watching the man for a couple of months already. However, she hadn't learned much about him. More than once, his handsome face had made her heart pound only a bit faster. That had never happened to her before, although she had had the chance to encounter some more beautiful male specimens.

She shook off the inappropriate thoughts. Still, her fingers lingered over the man's forehead, and she brushed a dark brown lock of hair away.

"Do you think you can stand?" she asked him quietly. Her voice didn't betray her thoughts or the compassion she felt at the sight of his bloody and bruised face.

The man didn't answer but touched his mouth with shaky fingers and checked his teeth gingerly. Apparently, he wasn't sure that he hadn't lost one of them in the heat of the fight.

"Listen to me," the policewoman grabbed his hand with determination and squeezed it to draw his attention. "You can check your various aches and wounds later. We have to move out of here and fast. Those guys might come back with reinforcements, and this time, they might also bring weapons with them. You're done for the day, mister, and I am only one, so we should start cracking. I assume that you want to see the sun tomorrow morning," she snapped at him.

"Of course, if you can see anything tomorrow," she grumbled, changing her position. One of her calf muscles had begun to cramp.

The woman placed herself at the man's back and slid her hands beneath his arms. Then, she began to push him up. The man had finally decided to help her when he heard that his attackers might return to finish the job. He didn't have the wish to end up thrown into Lake Ontario or at the bottom of the foundation of a new building.

Now that she had his cooperation, the policewoman managed to help the man stand up. He was over six feet tall and towered over her. The woman shook her head in dismay when she realized how heavy he was.

"Let's see how we can leave this God-forsaken place now," she mumbled and propped the man, placing her shoulder under his arm. The man left his weight on her, and she stumbled. Both practically fell to the ground.

"Oh, oh, oh," she cried out, and her legs shook because of the effort. "My God, you're like dead weight, man. You're heavier than a sack of grains," she mumbled after she straightened and regained her balance.

"I know it won't be easy, but let's try to get to my car only in one piece. I don't feel like being flattened on the pavement with you on top of me. You'll have to cooperate with me, man," she barked at him. "Don't think that they won't come back," she warned the man, piercing him with her narrowed eyes. "None of us will fare well if they return before we could fly the coop."

The man nodded. However, he didn't seem very convinced of her words. In fact, his ears rang, and a weird hum buzzed in his brain. Still, he made an effort to move a foot in front of the other.

The woman started panting in no time at all. She shook her head, wondering at the man's dead weight on her shoulders. She also cursed herself, wondering why she had parked the car so far away from the back alley of the casino. She should have thought that she might need it sooner or later.

Trying to take her thoughts off the herculean effort she was making, she asked, "What's your name?"

In fact, the policewoman knew the man's name and was afraid that she might pronounce it unwillingly. She decided against shocking the guy into prostration by calling him by his name right then. They still had to cover some distance to her car, and she needed him focused on that task.

The man turned his head toward her slowly and gazed at her through the slit of the one eye he still could use. He answered only after a long minute, and the woman had already given up hearing an answer from him.

"I'm Jay. And you?" he asked in a gruff tone of voice.

"I'm Ellen," the woman replied. "Nice to meet you, Jay. Or maybe it's not so nice for you after all," she made an attempt to shrug but gave up immediately. The man's proximity didn't leave her too much room for maneuver.

"Hmm. I wouldn't say such a thing," Jay replied. "I'm actually thrilled to meet you, Ellen. But for you, I'd have ended a corpse in the lake. I bet my last packet of cards on that," he assured her.

"Even now, you're thinking of cards," Ellen shook her head.

"How would you know what I usually think?" the man asked her, raising an eyebrow high on his forehead.

That was quite a feat, considering his already deformed face, and Ellen admired him for that. However, Jay hissed afterward. Apparently, it hadn't been such a smart move, after all.

A fleeting smile appeared on Ellen's lips, but she chased it away. "I have been watching you," she admitted when they got closer to her car. She thought she would manage to drag him from there if she had to.

"You've been watching me," Jay whispered with disbelief. "Since when?" he asked and halted, and the woman lost her balance for a few seconds.

"For a while," Ellen answered with indifference once she regained her footing. "Here we are," she stopped the man's next question. "That's my car," she pointed toward a dark blue car at the end of the parking lot. "At least, I was smart enough to park here, at the edge of the lot," Ellen scowled. "Move your feet, and let's get there."

With a lot of effort, the woman loaded Jay into the car. She propped him back in the car seat and then fastened his seatbelt with nimble fingers.

Jay's eyes stared at her small and delicate hands in awe. *'So graceful and yet so strong at the same time,'* he shook his head, a gesture he regretted in a second.

"I think I should take you to the hospital," Ellen said to him. Her eyes swept over his features with concern. She was worried that he might have a concussion, if not a fracture of the jaw.

The man tried to shake his head again and refute her proposition but groaned instead, and his shaky fingers touched his head gingerly.

"No hospital," he hissed through his clenched teeth.

"Maybe you should look in the mirror before making this decision," Ellen replied in a dry tone of voice. "I doubt that you are in the appropriate frame of mind to make any choice in the matter," she inferred in a stern tone of voice.

"No hospital," Jay groused and tried to stare Ellen down. Still, with one of his eyes swollen shut and the other a narrow slit, his stare had no effect. "I'll be fine," he mumbled without too much conviction.

"All right then, cowboy. Let's take you home, then," Ellen shrugged with indifference. If he didn't care about what had happened to him, she didn't see why she would have worried.

The woman glanced behind her toward the alley, making sure that none of the thugs had come back out. Satisfied that the lane was still empty, she ran around the hood and opened the driver's side car door with a brusque gesture. Her eyes swept the shadowed road once more, and then, she sat down in the car seat and blocked the car doors with a sigh of relief. They were almost out of trouble.

Ellen glanced at Jay again, and her heart shrank when she noticed that he had sagged in his seat. She pursed her lips and started the car, driving out of the parking lot with a screech of wheels.

The woman drove at the maximum legal speed and didn't stop until she had encountered the first traffic lights. Jay groaned when she braked the car suddenly, but Ellen didn't pay any attention to him. She drummed her fingers onto the steering wheel. Her gaze swept the interior of the car that stopped next to her on the right lane. When she ensured that none of the casino owner's enforcers were in that car, she turned his eyes to Jay and measured him thoughtfully.

When the green of the traffic lights flashed, Ellen started the car and practically pressed the speed pedal to the floor. She continued on straight ahead for about two hundred yards. Then, Ellen changed direction toward the lake area.

Jay turned his head to the woman and steadily levelled his stare on her. "Where are we going?" he asked her in a light tone of voice, although his right hand had clenched into a fist.

"You said that you didn't want to go to the hospital," Ellen pointed out. "So, I'm driving you home," she explained.

"Whose home?" Jay insisted, pronouncing the words through his tightened teeth. Various pains started to make themselves known now. Before, the adrenaline had stifled them.

"Yours," Ella replied with indifference, without turning his eyes toward him. They had already gotten far from the casino, but she didn't put it beyond the casino owner to send someone after them. She was busy watching the street and the mirrors at the same time.

"And how would you know where I live?" Jay gritted his teeth and straightened up in the car seat despite his protesting body. He found that the whole situation was dubious.

"I just told you that I had been watching you," Ellen shrugged and turned onto York Street. She knew that Jay lived there in a high-rise building. "I'm a police officer. Of course, I checked you out and followed you a few times," she explained to him in an even tone of voice as if she had explained basic things to a child. She didn't divulge the fact that she hadn't found too much about him.

"What the heck?" Jay groused. "Why would you follow me? What did you think you would find out?" the man asked with bewilderment. As far as he knew, his life wasn't out of the ordinary, and no one outside his family knew about his genetic heritage and his half-gifts.

Ellen shrugged again and led her car toward the visitors' parking lot next to Jay's building. "I had to know who you were and in what kind of business you were involved in."

She braked and turned to him with a half-smile, "Let's take you home, big guy. There, we will see what I can do for you, and if you still have questions, I will also answer them."

"I do hope that's a euphemism," Jay mumbled and unfastened his seat belt with not very sure fingers.

"I'll pretend I haven't heard you," Ellen replied in a severe tone of voice. "Wait until I get to your door. I would hate it to see you sprawled on the pavement. I think it would be easier to prop you than to pick you up," she warned him and got out of the car.

She didn't know how stubborn the man was, so she hurried to get to his side and sighed with relief. Jay hadn't tried to get out of the car but waited for her.

'At least he's got some brains in that handsome head of his,' she reflected, opening his door. *'Of course, he doesn't look so handsome now, though,'* she observed with regret.

Ellen gave her hand to Jay and waved at him to grab her arm. "Throw your legs out of the car first," she advised him. "Lean onto me, and I will help you stand up."

Jay grimaced when he moved his legs. He was sure he would see the imprint of those thugs' boots on his thighs and calves. He grabbed Ellen's arm with one hand and pushed himself out of the car with a deep groan.

Ellen braced her legs to support Jay's weight and held him until he could stand. When she was sure that he wouldn't fall on his already broken nose, the young woman waved to him to lean onto the car so that she could close the door. Then, she took his arm over her shoulders, and they started the arduous walk toward the front door of the building.

"I suppose this is one of those expensive buildings with a front desk in the lobby," Ellen said. "I haven't been inside," she admitted.

"You suppose well," Jay replied dryly. The man didn't feel at ease knowing she had been watching him for a while.

When they got to the entrance, Ellen sighed. As she suspected, they needed a keycard to get inside.

"Do you still have your keycard?" she inquired.

Jay patted his jacket pocket, "Yep, it is right here."

Ellen rolled her eyes and shook her head. "Do you think the door will open if the key card remains in your pocket?" she asked him.

"Don't be mean," he mumbled and took the keycard out of his pocket and handed it to her. "My brain is foggy," he groused. "I thought you'd show more compassion for my present state."

"You're like this because of your bad habits, not because of me," she retorted in a stern tone of voice.

"Bad habits?" Jay inquired with bewilderment. "What bad habits?"

"You know very well that I'm talking about your gambling," Ellen pointed out. "That's addictive and unhealthy, as you found out tonight," she lectured.

"Thanks, mother," Jay said through his teeth. "I'll keep that in mind."

"You'd better do," Ellen didn't yield. "Next time, I might not be there to get you out of trouble."

"Until then, will you open that damned door?" Jay asked in a sarcastic tone of voice. "I feel like I'm collapsing, and believe me, I've never felt this way before," he warned her.

Ellen shook her head, and her ponytail jumped and touched Jay's chin. A faint smell of wildflowers teased the man's nose, and Jay inhaled deeply.

CHAPTER TWO

After a strenuous walk through the lobby of the building under the front desk attendant's baffled expression, they shared a somewhat relaxed trip with the elevator to the 27th floor. Ellen merely propped Jay on the sidewall of the cabin, and she took the opportunity to catch her breath. She just held the man upright with one hand.

The sixty-five feet from the elevator to Jay's apartment took them a little longer. Once inside, Ellen led the man to the large sofa in the living room and helped him sit down.

Jay sagged on the couch and leaned his head on the backrest, his hands on his thighs. He sighed with relief, and his fingers twitched on his legs, drawing Ellen's attention.

Her eyes lingered over the man's muscular thighs for a few moments, and then she shook her head to clear it. Ellen observed his chest to make sure that his breathing wasn't obstructed. However, to her dismay, the man seemed unable to draw deep breaths into his lungs. She needed to focus on other things.

"Jay, don't fall asleep," she ordered to him in an authoritative tone of voice, and leaning over him, she shook his shoulder.

The man opened his only sound eye and annoyedly stared at the woman. Jay was tired and ached everywhere. Unconsciousness seemed very attractive to him right then. He imagined that he wouldn't have felt anything if he had fallen asleep.

"What now?" he asked in a huff, staring at Ellen because he couldn't see her accurately. Besides, the woman might have been willowy but proved extremely bossy, and he didn't like that too much right then. On the one hand, he wanted Ellen there with him. On the other, Jay believed that he would have preferred to see the back of her.

"I'm sorry, big boy, but you need to take your clothes off," Ellen replied with regret in her voice, the tips of her fingers brushing fleetingly off the side of his face.

Jay's lips twitched with repressed amusement. Then, he schooled his features not to show anything. "I'm sorry, too, sweetie. I won't say that you aren't tempting. That would be a lie. You're tempting like hell, but I'm afraid that I'm not able to do anything right now," he explained, his voice filled with sorrow.

"Do you want to make me forget that you're already battered and kick you?" Ellen asked with annoyance, drawing back, and one of her eyebrows hiked up her forehead.

"You wouldn't be so mean," he shook his head gingerly. The man's dizziness didn't allow him to make sudden gestures.

"Huh! Don't count on that," Ellen barked at Jay, and annoyance shone in her hazel gaze. "Take your clothes off. I need to see what happened to you. Then, we'll call an ambulance if it is necessary, regardless of what you're saying," Ellen warned him.

"I don't need an ambulance," Jay protested as firmly as he could. "You'll see that I'm fine," he assured Ellen and tried to take his jacket off.

But then, his fingers refused to listen to him, and he couldn't unfasten the two buttons which he still had on his jacket. The others had been torn off during the fight.

Ellen sighed and leaned over him. She did short work of unbuttoning his jacket. The woman pulled Jay toward her and removed the coat when she finished with that, turning a deaf ear to his groans with obstinacy. *'I can't think that he hurts. I have to see in what state he is.'*

Ellen had already seen the outward results of the savage beating inflicted on him. She knew that the goons had broken the man's nose and cracked his lips. She was interested in his rib cage now.

The woman urged him to remain in the same position, with his head on her shoulder, until she took off his shirt as well. She checked his back first and grimaced when her eyes fell on some huge angry bruises.

'Those guys knew where to kick him,' Ellen thought, shaking her head with annoyance. *'Poor guy will pee with blood for a couple of days,'* the young woman reflected, and afterward, she pushed Jay with care toward the backrest. Then, she straightened and brushed the tips of her fingers over his bruised chest and ribs.

"I like that," the man mumbled. "If you don't press too hard, it's quite enjoyable. Don't stop," he pleaded.

Ellen's eyes lifted swiftly at the man's face. Angry words climbed up her tongue, and the woman was ready to scold him. But then, she noticed the mixture of pleasure and pain on his lips, and she kept quiet. Still, she pursed her lips and shook her head.

Ellen stepped back and said gently, "You need a doctor, Jay. No matter what you say," she continued, but he interrupted her.

"No doctor, Ellen, please. We'll call my sister. I trust her more than any other doctor."

"Is she a doctor?" Ellen inquired in a doubtful tone of voice.

"In a way," Jay replied with a quizzical smile on his lips. "My cell phone should be in the pocket of my jacket. Let's hope it survived," he added morosely.

Ellen picked up the jacket from where she had thrown it and patted the pockets. She found the cell phone, which seemed to still function, although the screen had fissured, and handed it to Jay. But then, he didn't look like paying any attention to her gestures. She sighed and asked, "What's your sister's name?"

"Maggie," Jay replied. "You will find her under Maggie."

"Good to know," Ellen retorted. "But before that, I would need your PIN to get into the phone menu," she observed with frustration.

"Oh, I forgot," he said softly, without bothering to open his eyes. "Just type 2611."

Ellen introduced the PIN, and the cell phone flashed to life.

"You've got quite a few missed calls and messages," she observed.

"Not important right now," Jay groused and waved his fingers.

Ellen looked at him and shook her head. Then, she opened the contacts and found Maggie's number in no time. She put the call through and handed the phone to Jay.

"Maybe you should talk to her," she observed with blatant sarcasm in her voice.

Jay just waved his hand negligently and said, "You can do it just fine." Gesturing with his fingers was the only movement he could do without feeling piercing pains everywhere.

The woman narrowed her eyes but didn't comment anymore. She waited patiently for someone to pick up the phone at the other end of the line. When the voicemail message entered, she covered the phone and asked, "Do you want to leave her a message?"

"Not really," he mumbled, a sign that he hadn't fallen asleep yet.

Ellen disconnected the call and braced her free hand on her hip. "So, we'll call the ambulance now," she decided, and her words stirred Jay into life.

He cracked the one eye that still opened a little and pierced her with a disgruntled look. "We could as well call Matt," he countered her proposition in a sulky voice.

"Is he a doctor?" Ellen inquired in a strained tone of voice. The worry for the man's physical state filled her with anxiety, and she had already lost her patience.

"Matt? No, he's a lawyer," Jay replied with another negligent wave of his hand. He had already shut his eye, and a smile fleeted on his lips.

"And how would a lawyer help you right now?" the woman snapped at him. "You can talk to him in the morning if you want to sue your attackers. Although I don't think you'd get anywhere with that. Tonight, you need medical care," she pointed out and stomped her foot onto the floor to drive her opinion home.

"I have gathered that," Jay replied peevishly. "Matt is a lawyer, but his wife used to be an EMT," he cracked his eye again to look at her.

Ellen concluded that she had had enough of feeling Cyclops's look on her and grimaced.

"If she was an EMT and isn't anymore, it means that she must not have been a good one, to begin with," she snorted, tilting her head meaningfully.

"That's not nice," Jay replied, upset, and his eyebrows bunched on his forehead.

"What? Telling the truth?" she inquired in a sweet tone of voice.

"That's not telling the truth. That's passing judgment without knowing the people involved. Nora isn't an EMT anymore because she was put on extended medical leave. A smart ass shot her while she was on the line of duty," Jay explained in a stern tone of voice to Ellen.

"Oh, I'm sorry," Ellen replied and blushed, embarrassed to have spoken without having all the information. "And can she have a look at you?"

"Of course, she can," he replied, and his tone of voice showed that the man was already sick of that fruitless conversation. "Just call Matt," he said through his locked teeth.

Ellen didn't comment. She knew that the man must have been in pain, which was why he reacted like a wounded wolf. She looked through Jay's cell phone contacts and found Matt's name immediately after Maggie's.

The woman said a little prayer in her mind that Matt would answer her call before putting the call through. She knew she would call the ambulance otherwise, and Jay would blow a gasket. *'Eh, I'll deal with that when the time comes,'* she reflected.

"Hey, Jay. What's up?" a masculine grave voice came on the line. "I called you earlier, but you didn't pick up."

"I apologize for bothering you, sir," Ellen began to say. "I..."

"What the heck? Where did you find this cell phone?" the man's voice thundered on the line, interrupting her reply.

Ellen sighed profoundly and grimaced. She recognized the voice of a man used to giving orders. Her eyes flew to Jay as if she looked for support from him. However, he had already leaned his head on the backrest of the sofa. Jay didn't seem to pay attention to anything.

"I didn't find the phone, sir," she replied in a challenging tone of voice as well. She dealt with men like him on any given day, after all. "I am with your brother in his apartment, but he's a bit... under the weather, let's say, and that's why I'm calling you."

"What have you done to him?" Matt's voice thundered a bit louder.

"I've saved his ungrateful hide," she huffed.

"And you need money?" Matt asked with scorn.

"Listen here, mister, and listen good," Ellen's voice raised a notch. "I haven't called you to take potshots at me. Your brother needs medical help. He refused to go to a hospital, and now, he refuses that I called an ambulance. Jay says that your wife is an EMT. That's why I called you," she ended her angry tirade.

"I apologize," Matt answered in a calmer tone of voice. "We'll be there in about ten minutes. Is it all right?" he inquired.

"Yes, that's okay," Ellen replied, relieved that she wouldn't be alone with the wounded man anymore, and someone who knew what to do to him would come.

"You'll stay there until we come," Matt ordered to her, and she grimaced again.

"Not because you've ordered me to stay," she pointed out. "I would have stayed anyway. I haven't finished my business with your brother yet."

"And what business would that be?" Matt asked with suspicion.

"That's between the two of us, Jay and me. It's none of your business," she replied in a grumpy voice and disconnected the call rudely.

"Yeah, Ellen, what business would that be?" Jay's voice reached her ears, and she turned her eyes to him.

"So you haven't been sleeping," she concluded.

"Nah, I can't. To be honest, everything hurts. I'd welcome fainting right now, but it seems that it's not in the cards for me," Jay waved his hand.

Ellen shook her head and placed the cell phone on the coffee table. "What's with you and the cards? Why are you so obsessed with them?"

Jay shrugged and hissed immediately. "Damn, that hurts. To answer your question, the only things I can see with clarity are the cards," he replied in a tone filled with pain.

"What do you mean?" Ellen tilted her head in confusion.

"That is an answer for another time," he replied with a sigh.

CHAPTER THREE

Matt kept his promise and rang at Jay's intercom ten minutes later. Recognizing the man's voice, Ellen pressed the key to let him come upstairs, and in a few minutes, he knocked on Jay's door.

Ellen opened the apartment door for him, and to her surprise, she found herself before a group of four people. Her eyebrows shot up on her forehead, and her eyes shifted from one person to the other.

The woman held the door open with one hand, but she didn't step back to allow them to come inside. The two guys and two women looked back at her with curiosity. She took her time to peruse every one of them at length, which brought various expressions on the visitors' features.

First, Ellen's eyes swept over a dark-haired man, whose mouth had pursed, showing his discontent because she kept him at the door. *'So what?'* she reflected and shrugged inwardly.

Ellen found the man quite tall and broad-shouldered. Still, she admitted that he didn't have the bulk of the other one. When she shifted her eyes to the second guy, a massive blond-haired man, she noticed that he had fixed his icy blue eyes on her without even blinking. The scar running along the side of the man's face spoke of a checkered past, and Ellen's eyes widened slightly.

'Hmm, I shouldn't wonder at what kind of company Jay's keeping,' she reflected with sarcasm. 'He's a gambler, after all.'

Still, the thought that she judged Jay without having all the facts nudged at her. Usually, she wouldn't rush in passing judgment or making opinions before having the entire picture.

But then, when it came to Jay, Ellen wasn't very clear-headed. The man had touched a particular spot in her heart since she laid her eyes on him for the first time. However, the woman refused to analyze her reactions and feelings toward Jay too close, afraid of what she might discover.

Ellen noticed that the giant held a honey-blond woman's hand in his, while the dark man's arm was around a redhead's shoulders. Their gestures stirred her envy, although she couldn't say precisely why. Ellen's eyes went from one to the other once more, and one of her eyebrows rose inquiringly.

"I'm Matt," the dark-haired men informed her when a couple of minutes passed, and she hadn't said or done anything. His dark blue eyes pierced her openly, and then, he stretched his hand to Ellen. "We talked over the phone," he reminded her. He hoped that she would quit examining them as if they had been exhibits in a museum, and she would move aside so that they could enter the apartment. He didn't feel like plowing through her to get to his brother.

"I'm Ellen," she shook the man's hand. "And yes, I remember that we talked on the phone. I see you've brought reinforcements," she observed with malice, and the corners of her mouth lifted. "Were you afraid I'd subdue both you and your wife single-handed?"

Matt's eyes narrowed, and his lips pursed even more when the woman's words registered in his mind. The blond massive guy's lips twitched, but he suppressed his amusement and intervened before Matt could have snapped at the woman.

"I'm sure that Matt's intentions were different. Actually, we were spending time together tonight, so we decided to come with Nora and Matt."

Ellen waved the man's concerns away with a negligent gesture and invited them to come inside. She closed the door behind them and then said, "Jay is still on the sofa, as you can see," she pointed to the living room. "I convinced him to lie down because I didn't think that sitting up would help him too much. I also packed some ice in a couple of towels, and despite his grumbling, I placed them on his face," she turned to Nora, guessing that she was the EMT. "You'll see that one of his eyes is completely shut, and the other is almost there too. I haven't found anything else but ice in his freezer. Probably, he doesn't eat at home," she shrugged.

"Yep, that's Jay," the woman with the honey-coloured hair replied with a wide smile. "Matt seems to have forgotten to introduce us. I'm Becka, by the way. This one here is my husband, Bryan," she put her small hand on the giant's chest. "Matt, you've already talked to, and of course, this is Nora, his wife," she pointed toward the redhead.

"I'm Ellen," the woman replied and smiled back at Becka.

It was impossible for Ellen not to like the petite young woman. She gave the impression that she had just finished high school. The woman seemed open, and her chocolate eyes were

25

filled with warmth. Ellen didn't understand how Becka and Bryan had ended together, but she had seen stranger things in her lifetime.

Ellen shook everyone's hand, and then, impatiently, she turned to Nora, bracing her hands on her hips. "Don't you think you should check Jay up?" she asked her in a demanding tone of voice, tilting her head toward Jay's body lying on the sofa.

Matt's eyebrows bunched on his forehead. The man didn't know what to think of that slip of a woman. However, Matt didn't like her bossiness too much.

Nora laid her hand on his arm and stopped any comment he wanted to make. Matt turned his eyes to her, and his wife shook her head and whispered to him, "Don't take it personally. She only worries about your brother."

"His nose is broken," Ellen informed them in an impatient tone of voice. "I think some of his ribs are cracked. His breathing is shallower than I would like," she gesticulated.

"Don't worry," Bryan quieted her by placing a hand on her shoulder. "Jay is strong, and he'll recover soon, you'll see. I will take care of his nose," he added in a soothing tone of voice.

Ellen drew back, and her eyes widened when she heard his words. "What do you mean?" she asked, and anxiety made her voice shake. The woman didn't think that she would like Bryan's taking care of Jay's nose.

"I'll just put it back," the giant shrugged and went closer to the sofa.

Still, Ellen stepped in front of him and stopped him. "I don't think so. I won't let you hurt him more than he is," she snapped at him.

The corners of Bryan's mouth turned up. He bit his upper lip and asked dryly, "And how would you stop me from snapping his nose back?"

"With my gun, if I need to," she retorted with determination.

"Don't fret so much, Ellen," Jay's voice came from behind her, and she turned to him. "Bryan knows what he's talking about. I imagine it would hurt like hell, but what the heck," he shrugged. "It hurts now."

"Are you sure?" Ellen asked him with hesitation. "I won't let him touch you if you don't want it," she reassured Jay.

"I'd like to see that," Jay mumbled. "Unfortunately, I can't see too much right now," he said ruefully.

Nora closed the distance between her and Ellen and touched the woman's arm. "Don't worry, Bryan won't hurt him. The nose must be set back, or Jay will remain with a crooked nose, and it will still hurt. Allow me to take a look at him," she urged the woman to move aside so that she could get to Jay.

"What the heck?" Matt interceded in a stern tone of voice. "I'll remove her if it is necessary."

Ellen glanced at him sideways. She braced her hands on her hips and straightened her shoulders.

"Try that, big guy. Let's see how well you fare against me."

"She's got grits," Jay noticed, and Bryan burst into laughter.

Becka nudged her husband in his ribs. "Shut up, Bryan."

"But I didn't say anything," he protested.

Jay removed the towels off his face with a groan. "All right. You've had enough fun, all of you. This waiting to be examined is killing me. Let's get to work, people," he ended his tirade in a near whisper.

Ellen rushed to him and brushed the tips of her fingers over his forehead. "Does it hurt worse now?" she asked him in a gentle tone of voice.

"Somewhat," Jay admitted and put his hand over hers to keep it where it was. The woman's hand was cold and smooth, and it felt good.

The other four watched the interaction between the two young people with curiosity, and Matt's eyebrows shot up with amazement.

"When did you two meet?" he asked because he couldn't hold his curiosity at bay.

Ellen jumped up guiltily, and Jay groaned. "You had to open your big mouth," Jay reproached his brother. "You have never known when to keep it shut," he observed with another moan.

"All right, let's take a look at you," Bryan said.

"You're not the EMT," Ellen remarked dryly.

"But he knows how a battered body looks like," Jay replied.

"I don't doubt that," Ellen showed her agreement with his assessment.

Becka frowned and intervened in an angry voice, which Ellen wouldn't have expected of her. "Bryan is a fighter and a trainer. Whatever else you might think of him, it is plain wrong."

Ellen put her hands up and replied, "I didn't mean any disrespect."

"You did," Bryan said quietly. "But that's not important now," he observed, leaning over Jay to take a closer look at his wounds, and Nora followed him.

Suddenly, the place around Jay became crowded. Still, Ellen didn't abandon her position and kept a sharp look at Bryan's ministration. The man touched the blackened spots around Jay's eyes. Jay groaned again, and Ellen's hands curled into fists. Her mouth pursed, and apprehension sparkled in her eyes.

"Yep, you won't see much for a few days," Bryan concluded. "Some steaks would be good. They would diminish the swelling," he explained.

"I'm going out and buy some," Matt said. "There's a Metro close to here, and it is open twenty-four hours."

"Do that," Bryan turned his head to him. "Considering what Ellen told us, maybe you should buy some food as well. Jay won't be able to go out for a couple of days or even more. You should get something that he could eat without too much trouble. If I remember well, Jay's as good at cooking as you are," he added with a smile, and Nora and Becka laughed. "Of course, I can make something for him now that I'm here and come back with more homemade food tomorrow," Bryan offered, but Ellen shook her head.

"It isn't necessary. I know my way in the kitchen, and I can take care of his food."

The other four people looked at her nonplussed, and Jay grinned. He liked the way she was thinking.

Matt nodded with a frown and then turned to his wife. "I'll be back soon, love." He kissed her lips, and then, he lifted her hand and brushed his mouth over her fingers as well.

Ellen tried not to look, but the man's actions fascinated her. She turned back to Bryan when she felt his eyes on her, and she blushed. Bryan grinned and went back to examining Jay while Matt left the apartment.

"Yep, your nose is broken, Jay," Bryan concluded. "Hold your breath," he advised his friend, and with a sudden move, he straightened the man's nose.

Ellen winced when the sickening noise filled the room, and her hand grabbed Jay's as if she wanted to give him support. Jay groaned deeply, and tears appeared in the corners of his eyes.

"See, it's done," Bryan lifted his eyes to Ellen and noticed the paleness of her face. "I'm sorry, but he's better now," he said softly.

Ellen merely nodded, biting her lips, and her fingers flexed over Jay's. "What about his ribs?" she inquired in a small voice.

"They're just bruised, in my opinion," Bryan said and turned to Nora.

Nora brushed her hands over Jay's chest and sides, and then, she nodded in agreement. "Of course, an x-ray might be more accurate than our assessment," she said, lifting her eyes to Jay, who shook his head.

"No hospital," the man groused. "X-rays mean hospital."

"But if your ribs are broken...," Ellen started to say, but Jay shook his head and groaned. His head still hurt, and the humming inside his brain intensified whenever he moved it.

"All right," Bryan decided, "we'll bind the ribs tightly, and he should be better in a couple of days, even if his ribs have fissures. They'd do the same at the hospital," he shrugged.

"Do that," Jay agreed.

Still, Ellen hesitated a few seconds. She wasn't sure that Jay should skip the hospital if his ribs were hurt. Nora touched her hand and said, "He'll be fine. Bryan is right."

Ellen shifted her eyes to Bryan, who was still waiting for her answer. She nodded, and the shadow of a smile appeared on Bryan's lips.

"Do you have some bed sheets you won't miss too much?" he turned to Jay afterward.

"I have a white set. My mother bought the others, and she would have my head if you ruin them," he warned Bryan.

"I'm going to look into your linen closet," Becka announced and left the living room.

Ellen watched after her with curiosity. She didn't understand why Becka knew Jay's apartment so well.

"She's Jay's cousin," Bryan informed her quietly, and Ellen blushed, uncomfortable to see that the man could scan her mind without effort.

"When you don't guard your features, your face is very expressive, and your thoughts are easy to read," Bryan explained to her with a grin.

"Good to know," Ellen replied in a strained tone of voice, upset with herself that she had lost her focus, thus allowing the giant to see what was going on in her mind.

Becka returned with a white sheet and handed it to Bryan. "Do you need scissors?" she asked him, and her husband grinned. He shook his head, and taking the sheet off her hand, he made short work of tearing it.

"This will also hurt, big boy," he warned Jay, pulling him in a sitting position. Bryan turned a deaf ear to Jay's groans. "Quit being a sissy," he grumbled at the man.

Ellen sat next to Jay on the sofa and took his hand. At the same time, she frowned at Bryan, considering his bedside manner inappropriate, given Jay's condition.

"You shouldn't scold him. He's hurt," Ellen snapped at Bryan.

"Huh!" Jay exclaimed. "As if you hadn't treated me the same way," he observed maliciously.

"We had to hurry then," the woman replied. "If you remember, those five goons could have come back to finish the job."

"So, you battled five guys," Bryan surmised.

"More or less," Ellen answered to him. "More likely, those guys pummeled him. He was down for the count in no time at all," she informed Bryan, and Jay grimaced.

"You have a big mouth too," he concluded, and Ellen just shrugged.

"I told you that you should come to the dojo," Bryan shook his head. "You need to know to protect yourself, man."

"Especially with your line of work," Ellen interceded again.

"Will you shut up?" Jay snapped at her, furious now.

"What line of work?" Becka inquired.

"Nothing," Jay waved his hand negligently. "Just something that got into her hard head."

"Don't tell me you started gambling again," Becka frowned at him. "You've taken a beating before because of that. Haven't you learned your lesson yet?"

"Quit lecturing me, mother," Jay mumbled. Too tired and in too much pain, he didn't feel like listening to anyone's wise words.

Bryan shook his head to Becka, letting her understand that she wasted her breath. Then, with Ellen's help, he started binding Jay's ribs tightly, paying no heed to the man's grunts. Jay was utterly spent and lay back down on the sofa when he finished.

"Wouldn't you prefer the bedroom?" Becka asked him.

The man just fluttered his fingers in denial and sighed with relief that the tormenting session had ended.

"You will have to hold the slices of meat on your face," Bryan advised him. "I know the smell is awful, but the raw meat will help in the long run."

Jay waved his hand again without making any commitment at all. Bryan's face hardened, but Ellen said, "I will take care of that, no worries."

"Are you going to remain here over the night?" Nora inquired with bewilderment.

"Yes, I will," Ellen replied, and her tone of voice challenged any one of them to refute her claim of staying there with Jay.

"All right then," Bryan approved of her decision. "You'll need to check on him at least a couple of times during the night. Do you know how to check and see if there's a problem as a result of a concussion?"

Ellen nodded quietly, and she brushed her fingers through Jay's hair again. The other three people looked one at the other meaningfully.

"What should we say to Aunt Marjorie, Jay?" Becka asked afterward, and the man winced.

"Nothing. Don't even mention my name. Don't remind her of my existence for a few days, all right?" his words stumbled one after the other.

"Who's Aunt Marjorie that you're so agitated hearing her name?" Ellen inquired, perceiving his distress.

"His mother," Nora informed her with a smile in her tone of voice. "She would be all over him if she found out what had happened to him," she explained.

"That's why I wanted Maggie," Jay muttered again. "She knows to keep her mouth shut."

"And we don't?" Bryan's left eyebrow lifted.

"You do, but the others don't," Jay retorted angrily.

"Nice of you," Becka slapped him over the shoulder, and Ellen's eyes rounded. "Don't worry," Becka told her. "He hasn't felt a thing. Anyway, Maggie isn't in Toronto, Jay. She called you earlier to tell you that she was going toward the north."

"What the heck is she doing there?" Jay cracked his eye, surprised by Becka's news.

"That she didn't say," Becka shook her head. "You know, Maggie. She likes to play everything close to the vest. She said that she wouldn't have cell phone coverage there. Otherwise, she would have called you already. She must have felt that you were in trouble."

"How could she?" Ellen wondered, and her eyes widened.

"They're twins," Bryan informed her in a dry tone of voice.

"Ah, I see," she replied. The woman had heard that twins usually shared a close connection, and she didn't question the validity of Bryan's statement.

"Where the heck did Matt go?" Jay asked. He didn't like that the others offered Ellen too much information.

"Don't fret like an old woman," Becka retorted. "He'll be back soon."

"Can't we wait for him without making conversation?" Jay asked them, staring them down through the narrow slit of his eye.

"Oh, now, I see what the problem is," Becka laughed. "You'd better not upset me, Jay. I'll tell Ellen everything I can otherwise."

Jay waved his hand toward her rudely and closed his eye, resigned that he didn't have any control over the situation. He didn't worry overmuch, though. He knew that Becka couldn't divulge too much. The rules couldn't be broken.

CHAPTER FOUR

J ay woke up with a groan and rubbed his forehead with the tips of his fingers. The man wanted to rub his eyes, as well. Luckily, he immediately remembered what had happened to him and brushed his fingers through his hair instead. He made an effort to open his eyes, but one of them refused to listen to his commands stubbornly. Jay could see only a little through the other, and he swore a blue stream.

The bathroom door opened, and rushed steps across the wood boards reached his ears.

"Are you all right?" a soft female voice asked him, and Jay turned his head toward the sound.

Ellen's face came in his line of sight, and the man registered the worry in the woman's eyes and the rigid set of her mouth.

"Do I look all right?" he muttered, and Ellen curled her cold hand over the side of his face. Her touch soothed him instantly.

"I know you are in pain," she said softly, stroking his jaw carefully so that she wouldn't hurt him. "I'm pretty sure it is worse today than last night," she shook her head in sadness. "Matt brought you some Ibuprofen last night, and it might help you," she added.

"Yep, I'll take two or three right now," Jay decided on the spot. He hurt worse than the night before, and his ire escalated. His head felt three times bigger, and sharp pains pierced his nose and ribs.

Ellen laughed and shook her head. "I'm sorry, big boy, but it doesn't work that way. You can't have more than one pill, and only after you've eaten something.

"Do you think I can eat right now?" Jay groused, and his eyebrows bunched over his eyes in annoyance. "My jaw hurts, and I'm afraid that at least one of my teeth is moving."

"However, you will still eat," Ellen said in a stubborn tone of voice. "I'm going to prepare a bowl with oatmeal for you to eat."

"Who made you the boss?" the man asked, annoyed with her high-handed manner.

"You, when you got beaten in the middle of a dark alley and couldn't find your way out from there," she replied dryly.

"Nice," Jay observed. "You'll remind me of that for the rest of my days," he said with bitterness.

"Why not?" Ellen shrugged. "No one pushed you to play cards in a den of thugs. Now, you have to suffer my nasty rebukes."

"Don't you have anything else to do? Anywhere else to be?" Jay asked. However, he knew that he proved ungrateful and a liar. In fact, he liked having the woman around. She was easy on the eye and terribly tempting. His fingers itched to run through her honey-coloured mane or over her silky pale skin. Jay felt an odd fluttering in his gut whenever Ellen turned her hazel gaze to him, regardless that she only wanted to scold him.

"Not really," Ellen shook her head, and her words brought Jay back to the real world. "It's Saturday, so I'm free to do whatever I want, and I wish to bother you," she shrugged with nonchalance. "Now, stop grumbling, and let's get you to the bathroom. You'll feel better after a shower," Ellen slapped her hands to make him move.

Jay bad-mugged her and tilted his head. "I hope you don't think of giving me a bath," he said with bewilderment.

"Not really," she shook her head, blushing violently. "I do hope you can shower by yourself, and you won't require my help," she observed.

Jay grinned when he noticed the blush spreading over the woman's face. *'So this is the secret to making her pull back. I have to say something to embarrass her.'*

The man pushed himself off the couch, and his legs shook. He tensed, trying to keep his balance, and his ribs protested loudly. The man hissed.

"Are you sure that you're all right?" Ellen inquired with concern and got ready to catch him if he had fallen down. 'Only Lord knows if I survive if he falls over me,' she reflected.

She had already felt his weight on her and didn't think that she would be able to support him. However, the woman was determined to try because she couldn't let him fall and break his nose once more. *'I doubt he could go through Bryan's idea of medical care once more,'* she told herself.

Jay just waved her away, and with a hand supporting the right side of his torso, he started shuffling his feet toward the bathroom. He needed to brush his teeth and get rid of the metallic taste he had in his mouth. The man remembered that he had skipped that ritual the previous evening and didn't wonder about the offending tang on his tongue.

He also needed to check his teeth. Jay hoped that the constant ache in his jaw was due to bruised gums and not to an injured tooth. Jay had always hated going to the dentist, and therefore, he took great care of his teeth. One visit every half a year for cleaning was more than enough for him.

Ellen followed him. However, she kept a certain distance because she didn't want to put any wrong ideas into the man's head. Jay seemed prone to take everything in a specific way.

Jay shut the bathroom door in front of the woman and grinned mischievously. Ellen might have stepped lightly, but he was still aware that she was behind him. There were some things he had never shared with a woman and didn't feel like starting to do that right then.

Jay's relationships had always been shallow. They didn't go further than a night or two spent in the same bed with a particular woman. The man had taken care never to linger between a woman's bedsheets beyond dawn, and he never invited a woman into his sanctuary. Jay preferred to avoid complications.

The man didn't know how he felt about Ellen's presence in his house, and the fog in his brain didn't allow him to ponder the situation more. So, he put those thoughts aside and decided to take care of more urgent business.

Jay took a look at himself in the mirror and scowled. The range of colours and fist imprints on his face reminded him of an abstract painting. He had never been too fond of that art genre.

He turned his head this way and that way, tightening his teeth because of the discomfort those moves brought. Then, he concluded that Bryan had been right. *'Those unbelievably disgusting steaks have done their job,'* he nodded despite the dizziness that seized him immediately. Jay splashed his face with cold water and hissed, but then, the cold water soothed his bruises.

'I do have to start training with Bryan. Shame on me to need a girl to save my hide,' he scolded himself while brushing his teeth. *'At least, I still have all my teeth,'* he reflected, sliding his tongue over them. Luckily, only his gums had been harmed because of a well-placed fist. No teeth had been chipped or dislodged.

Jay turned to the shower stall and sighed deeply when he finished with that. Already exhausted, his legs shaking under his weight, he didn't feel like having a shower. *'Ellen seems capable of giving me a sponge bath if I don't take a shower,'* he thought and opened the glass door of the shower stall.

Suddenly, he stopped, tilted his head, and reflected, *'Would that be so bad? Nah... I'd better wash by myself. It's not so easy having her so close to me all the time. I'd better not invite more trouble,'* he decided and treaded purposefully into the stall.

CHAPTER FIVE

J ay stepped into the kitchen and saw Ellen. She was watching pensively out of the window, a cup of coffee in her hand. She seemed to have forgotten that she was holding it. Sensing his arrival, the woman turned to him and smiled.

"Now, you look much better," she admitted, her eyes sweeping over his still wet curly hair and the stubble covering his face. Ellen already knew that Jay didn't like to shave. She had seen him look like that before, and his dishevelled appearance wasn't just the result of his unpleasant encounter with five goons the previous night.

"That doesn't mean that I also feel better," Jay snapped at her. Her words didn't upset him. He was merely annoyed because the sunlight played with the woman's hair and put unhealthy thoughts into his head.

The shower had invigorated him and soothed some of his aches. Now, Jay moved with more ease, and the feeling that his legs had turned into spaghetti vanished.

He headed toward the island in the kitchen and propped himself onto one of the bar stools. Ellen had already set a bowl with oatmeal and a cup of coffee there. The man grimaced and eyed the content of the dish with suspicion.

"I'm not a toddler," Jay made a point of saying, turning his head toward Ellen and scowling at her.

The woman shrugged and returned to the table with supple steps, her eyes perusing the man's body with appreciation.

"Indeed, you're not a toddler," she replied. "Still, you complained that you couldn't eat anything hard. This was the only food appropriate for someone in your situation in the house. Take that up with your bossy brother. He bought the oatmeal. I had the impression that he even wanted to give me a list of instructions last night," Ellen couldn't refrain from expressing her discontent with Matt. However, she noticed that her comment didn't sit well with Jay. "And besides, adults eat oatmeal in the morning all the time. Almost all coffee shops offer it in their menu," Ellen pointed out, setting her cup on the top of the counter across from Jay.

"Well, I don't have it for breakfast," Jay replied stubbornly.

"I imagine you'd prefer to start your mornings with a tall glass of whiskey," she pierced the man with narrowed eyes.

"You seem to think the worst of me," Jay observed ruefully and shook his head gingerly. The dizziness hadn't left his head yet. Jay didn't feel like falling with his face in the bowl with oatmeal. Still, his edginess had gone up a notch since he woke up, and the man was sick of Ellen's constant putting down.

Ellen just shrugged and sipped from her coffee. "I might seem to think the worst of you, but let's be honest here, Jay. You do try your best to make me think like that," she waved her hand in the man's direction.

Jay decided to stuff his mouth with oatmeal. Apparently, he didn't do anything else but give more ammunition to the woman so that she could ambush him.

A fleeting smile flourished on Ellen's lips, but she turned her head because she didn't want Jay to see it.

"Your coffee is black," she remembered and turned back to him after a couple of seconds. "Would you like some sugar or milk?" she inquired.

Jay shook his head briefly and continued to eat the heap of oatmeal, which offended his senses. He would have liked a substantial breakfast, complete with eggs, sausages, and pancakes, even though the inside of his mouth still hurt. A sudden thought crossed his mind, and he looked at Ellen speculatively.

"Let's hear it," she tilted her head toward him. "I see you want something from me," she remarked.

"It's not much," Jay said in a small voice.

"Then you wouldn't hesitate to tell me what you wanted," she pointed out, raising her eyebrows in expectation.

"Well, what I want is not a big deal," Jay confessed. "The problem is that I don't know if you would accept it."

"All right, the suspense is killing me here," she urged him. "Spill it out."

"There's a nice cozy restaurant on Lower Simcoe Street. They have an amazing breakfast," Jay explained with enthusiasm. "You could go there and buy some for both of us. I'm sure this oatmeal doesn't seem really appealing to you either. I haven't seen any bowl in the sink or on the counter, so you haven't eaten any," he pointed out. "I'll give you my debit card. It's contactless, and you can pay with it."

Ellen watched him with suspicion for a few moments. "All right," she eventually said.

Relieved, Jay, who had been holding his breath, hoping for a positive response, sighed.

"But, I don't need your card," she made a point to mention. "I can pay for breakfast myself. However, I want your key," she presented her conditions.

"I want to buy breakfast, so I will pay," Jay said in a stern tone of voice, tapping his finger on the top of the counter. "And again, you have proved that you have an awful impression about me. Do you really think that I'm sending you to buy breakfast so that I could lock you out of my apartment?" he practically growled, hurt by Ellen's lack of trust.

Ellen just shrugged, "I wouldn't put it past you," she replied in a cold tone of voice, without any inflection.

"And that's just because you saw me playing cards a few times," Jay replied with bitterness, and his anger rose. "You know what? You're nothing but a hypocrite, haughty bitch," he hissed through his teeth, wanting to hurt her the way she had offended him.

"I haven't been calling you names," Ellen jumped off her barstool, her fists clenched on the sides.

"No, you haven't. You have a more subtle way of offending people," Jay replied with resentment. "I heard you pass judgment on everyone last night, and I have had enough of that. Forget about the dang breakfast. I don't need this sloppy oatmeal, either. I want you out of my flat now," he barked, getting off his chair, as well, and heading toward the living room, fed up with her opinions.

Ellen followed him, and he turned toward her like a bull. "I said that I want you out of here now," he practically roared. "Do I have to call the front desk to remove you from the premises?" he inquired in a biting tone of voice.

"We still need to talk," Ellen replied in a small voice.

Jay noticed the paleness of the woman's face and winced inwardly. He didn't know if he had frightened her with his behaviour, but he didn't bother to inquire about what she felt for the moment. He felt edgy, and tension vibrated in his blood. The man needed to be left alone.

"Some other time," he replied in a stern tone of voice. "I can't look at you right now. Maybe when you stop being such a judgmental bitch, we might have another type of conversation. For the moment, I have had enough."

Ellen winced at his words, and feeling somewhat guilty, she turned her eyes down for a few moments. The woman admitted that she had judged the man all the time, but that wasn't something she could have changed. To judge a gambler was in her blood. She couldn't think well about a player.

Gambling was an addiction. Ellen didn't have a soft spot for anyone addicted to something, regardless of whether it was drugs, gambling, drinking, or Lord knows what else. Despite Jay's harshness and her own guilt, she was determined not to yield before the man's demands, given the circumstances.

Ellen shook her head with stubbornness. "No, I can't leave you alone right now. You need my help. After I chased your brother away last night, telling him that I would take care of you, I simply can't leave, Jay. I am sorry, but I can't," she shook her head emphatically.

"Yeah, I see how you see to take care of me," Jay retorted with sarcasm. "No, thank you. I'm a big boy, as you keep saying. So, I'm pretty sure that I won't wither away if I remain alone. Quite the opposite. I might continue living outside a jail. I'm afraid that I will curl my fingers around your graceful neck and smother the life out of you," he snapped at her.

"Jay," she started saying, but the man put his hand up, stopping her words.

"Just get the hell out of here, Ellen. I thank you for last night. Yes, you have probably saved my sorry hide, I admit that. But right now, I don't want you here," he slashed the air with a sharp gesture, all his aches temporarily forgotten.

Ellen breathed deeply, and her fingers shook. She composed herself and schooled her features, not showing anything she was feeling. Then, the woman returned to the kitchen. She took her coffee cup off the counter and brought it to the sink. She washed the dish under Jay's stunned expression, and then she left the kitchen without a word.

Jay followed the woman out of the room and saw her picking up her bag off the coffee table, where she had left it the night before. Ellen didn't even spare a look at him. With a stone face, she just marched out of his apartment, closing the door quietly behind her.

Jay clenched his fists and locked his teeth in frustration. He didn't know what had come over him because it wasn't like him to lose his temper so swiftly. He slammed his right fist into the wall, "Damn, man!"

He swore viciously when the pain registered in his mind, and he ground his teeth. Then, the man closed his eyes for a few seconds, thinking of what he should do now that he was alone.

After pondering all the possibilities for a few moments, he picked up his cell phone off the coffee table. He found Matt's number in his contact list and dialled it. Matt picked up at once.

"Bring me some real breakfast," Jay ordered without bothering to greet his brother, and then he disconnected the call. He threw the phone back on the coffee table with irritation, and the phone slid and fell to the floor with a bang. Jay just shrugged. The screen had already been fissured the other night, so it didn't matter anymore. He would buy another one once he could go out into the world again.

The man strode to the sofa slowly and laid down carefully, like an old man, run down by arthritis. He covered his eyes with his arm and berated himself for losing his calm.

Jay regretted throwing Ellen out of his house in such an ugly manner. He loathed the fact that he had lost the chance of getting further with her. Besides the fact that the woman had saved his life, he actually liked her. Maybe a bit too much, the man reckoned.

CHAPTER SIX

J ay left the apartment building with a lively step and breathed deeply, welcoming the scented air into his lungs. In the last few days, he had spent some time on his balcony, watching and smelling the lake. But then, sitting on his balcony wasn't the same as walking among the people in the town. Even the air felt different, and the smells were sharper down in the street.

After being locked inside the apartment for over two weeks, he couldn't wait to stroll along the crowded streets of Toronto. He loved the pace of the nightlife in the big metropolis and the chance to encounter various groups of people. However, he also enjoyed the particular charm of the city on a Saturday morning.

Most people who knew Jay thought that the man represented a puzzle. Despite his profession, which invited him to solitude, he was, in fact, a social person.

Other artists like Jay spent their days locked in their houses, drawing away on the board and plotting their stories. His greatest joy was to mingle with various groups of people. Usually, he would go out every single day. Those outings fed his creative process.

His friends and acquaintances came from different avenues of life. Jay befriended intellectual guys who debated metaphysical and philosophical subjects. However, he had also made friends to a band of motorcycle aficionados, interested in braving the road and feeling the wind in their hair.

Jay had missed interactions with people during his recovery. He was sick and tired of his self-imposed seclusion. Jay hadn't dared to step out of the house and kept a low profile so that his mother wouldn't get a whiff of his sorry situation. Marjorie would have been all over him. Jay would have appreciated his mother's food, particularly her desserts. However, he wouldn't have felt comfortable with his mother's sideways looks toward his bruises and her quiet disapproval.

The man's thoughts had returned to Ellen with alarming frequency those last few days. Still, every time, Jay had found something else to do and occupy his mind, thus chasing those disturbing thoughts away. Once he became able to stand without pains and his vision improved, he went back to working on his comics.

Jay refused to think of Ellen, although his new addition to his characters strangely resembled her. He still hadn't forgotten either the woman's judgmental behaviour or veiled insults.

Nonetheless, that didn't mean that Jay wouldn't have liked to lay his eyes on Ellen again or listen to the sound of her voice. The woman was easy on the eyes and stirred Jay on a primal level, which frightened and thrilled him at the same time.

The other night, Jay hadn't succeeded in his struggle to push Ellen's face somewhere at the back of his mind. Her bluish-green eyes captivated him. Whenever Jay recalled how Ellen's hand had brushed his forehead, his belly hardened.

When he realized that he couldn't shake off the thoughts of Ellen anymore, Jay had resolved that he needed a change of scenery. He had to go out and do something else so that he would stop brooding.

The woman had been playing havoc with his system since the day he met her. Jay knew he was lying to himself when he claimed that he was happy to have thrown her out. He had actually regretted his gesture the moment the door closed behind Ellen.

Now, Jay didn't know where to find her, and he couldn't start looking for her in all the police stations. People would have thought he was a lunatic. So, it was easier to convince himself to believe that it was better for him that she had disappeared.

Anyway, it was definitely high time that he had left the house. His bruises had faded, and he moved easier now that his ribs had healed or almost healed. Just a twinge of pain pierced his body now and then, and that was only if he made sudden moves.

Once he had planned his next course of action, the man threw his dinner into the garbage bin with a nervous gesture and went to bed.

'That's it. I will go out tomorrow morning and have my life back. I refuse to let Ellen ruin my days.'

Jay had decided against taking his jacket and left the building only in a polo shirt. He had drunk his first coffee of the day on the balcony and seen that the sun promised another beautiful day.

The weather had swiftly changed since two days before. Once more, Toronto basked in a few surprising sunny summer days at the end of September.

His hands in his pants pockets, Jay strode with a supple gait through the people cruising the Harbourfront that Saturday morning. Everybody seemed bent on taking advantage of the hot day. They didn't doubt that rainfalls would follow soon enough, and their outings on the shore of the lake would be curtailed or would utterly cease.

Undecided, Jay stopped before a Tim Hortons. He would have liked to have some breakfast or brunch, but he wasn't very sure that he craved a sandwich from Tim's.

The man blocked the circulation for a few minutes, absently registering the sweet words that a group of young men directed to him. Jay shrugged with indifference. He had heard worse than that, after all.

Suddenly, he remembered Joe Bird's restaurant, so he turned on his heel and started that way. Jay doubted that he would be fortunate enough to find a seat on the patio at that hour on a Saturday, but he hoped for a change of luck. *It's high time my luck had changed,'* he gritted his teeth with frustration.

After a brisk walk to the restaurant, he found himself in front of a harassed hostess. Before he could expand on his wishes, the young woman had already informed him that the patio was packed.

Jay plastered the most attractive smile on his face, but the woman just looked at him blandly, unimpressed with his efforts.

"Come on," he tried to persuade her. "I'm sure that Kelly would help me if she were here," Jay said, congratulating himself that he remembered the other hostess's name. In reality, the man had visited the restaurant only twice or three times before, and he had stumbled on the same hostess by sheer luck.

His words didn't seem to affect the young woman, though. The hostess looked at him with condescension. She merely arched one perfectly groomed eyebrow and as if she had asked him, 'So what?'

Jay ground his teeth irate. He had to crush a vile curse, which climbed on his tongue, and he tightened his lips, piercing the young woman with a black look.

"Hey, man, welcome back," a young carrot-haired man thumped Jay's shoulder.

Jay turned his eyes to the man and recognized the waiter who had served him the last two times he had been in the restaurant.

"Apparently, I'm not so welcomed," Jay replied dryly, throwing a black look to the woman who had refused his admittance on the patio. "Your hostess can't be bothered to find a seat for me," he took care to mention, aware that he was plain mean, which he avoided in the regular course of events.

"Oh, Ann has just started working here, you know. She doesn't know our customers yet, so please, forgive her oversight," the guy hurried to say and waved his hand impatiently. "I will find you a seat immediately. The patio is indeed full. But will it be a problem if I seat you at a table with someone else? I have a table for four at the other end of the patio, and it's occupied only by a young woman," he informed Jay with enthusiasm and watched him expectantly.

Jay grimaced. He didn't feel like sharing a meal with an unknown woman, who would probably expect him to make some conversation. Precisely when he thought to refuse the man's offer and go somewhere else, his belly growled. That made him change his mind, and Jay nodded his assent.

Jay hadn't eaten his dinner the other night and had only one coffee that morning. He thought he would have some brunch out in town and didn't bother to see if there was anything left from what Bryan had brought for him the last time.

The waiter took a menu off the hostess's desk and invited Jay to come with him. Jay blessed the server's memory and nodded curtly toward the hostess, who watched him wide-eyed. Then, he followed the young man, who had started his winded stroll through the patio tables.

The waiter stopped at a table on the side with the lake at the far end of the patio. A woman was seated with her back to Jay, and his heart skipped a beat.

The woman's honey-coloured thick mane reminded him of Ellen. *'Damn, I can't get rid of her memory, not even here,'* he thought but continued to cover the distance between him and the table. Jay reached the table just in time to hear the woman's answer to the waiter's request.

"Yes, of course. I see it is full. I don't mind," the woman shrugged.

CHAPTER SEVEN

Now, Jay's right hand tightened into a fist. He couldn't forget that voice, and when the woman's face turned to him, he had the proof that his assumptions were correct.

'I'm cursed, that's it,' he reflected in dismay, and his eyes zeroed in on Ellen's features. *'I knew I was cursed, but I didn't realize that the damned curse extended in this area too,'* Jay corrected himself, recalling the curse that his great-grandmother had put on his head. His eyes narrowed with annoyance. But then, at the same time, he noticed that the woman's eyes widened, her lips parted slightly, and a slight blush pinked her face.

'Yep, sweetheart, it is me. At least, I'm not the only one taken by surprise here,' he thought. He nodded toward Ellen, a shadow of a smile turning the corners of his mouth up, satisfied with her reactions.

The woman attempted to say something, but she changed her mind and just nodded to him. She didn't seem capable of opening her mouth.

"Oh, you know each other," the server intervened with glee in his voice. "That's awesome, guys," he clapped his palms enthusiastically.

Jay had the impulse to slap the young man over the head. He didn't understand how the man could miss the signs of embarrassment on Ellen's face.

Still, he only shrugged because he couldn't do anything for her. He had been thinking way too much about her for the last few days. He felt the need to spare her the uneasiness, but that meant to leave her alone and walk away, and he couldn't do that.

"Take a seat, take a seat," the eager young man invited Jay with broad gestures. "Would you like that I bring you the same things that you ordered before?" he asked, and his eyes sparkled with hope.

Jay just nodded. He couldn't be bothered with reading a menu right at that moment. His eyes were busy sweeping all over Ellen.

The waiter left, rubbing his hands with delight. Jay might not have come to the restaurant too frequently, but he always gave a double tip whenever he did come. He recollected that Jay was a generous tipper.

Jay sat down across from Ellen and braced his elbows on the top of the table. Now, his eyes avoided Ellen's artfully and turned to the strip of sand and umbrellas beyond the rail separating the patio from the wooden board of the promenade. The lake glimmered in the sunlight a few yards farther, and white sails spotted the horizon.

'I need to go out on the lake. Matt could very well lend me his boat,' he reflected. *'If not, there's always Bryan,'* he concluded when he remembered that Matt was annoyed with him right then.

JAY'S SALVATION

The laughter of a couple of children mingled with the voice of a matron, who explained wisely the differences between two types of body lotions. A seagull cried out his discontent with a duck who stole a fish right from under his beak and then speared the air to look for another fishing spot.

From the corner of his eye, Jay observed Ellen at the same time. The woman seemed uneasy and edgy. She picked up her coffee cup off the table with a not very firm hand and lifted it to her lips.

"How have you been?" he chose that very moment to ask Ellen, shifting his eyes toward her suddenly.

Jay had the satisfaction to see the woman drop the cup, and the coffee splashed all over her red top. The dish broke with a loud sound, and the people from the tables around turned and stared at them. Jay didn't give any sign that their gazes impressed him. He didn't move his eyes from Ellen.

The woman's face turned scarlet, and she groaned in dismay. "Damn," she exclaimed, watching the disaster with wide eyes. "I've just bought this top," the woman mumbled with annoyance and grabbed a bunch of napkins, attempting to dry her blouse.

"The spots will still be visible," Jay shrugged, not moving a finger to assist her with anything. "That won't help you."

"Shut up, Jay," Ellen snapped at him and threw the napkins back on the table. She realized that he was right. She needed to wash the top to get rid of the spots.

The carrot-haired waiter appeared from thin air. He hurried to Ellen and Jay's table, ready to clean it.

"I apologize," Ellen looked up at him. "It simply slid from my fingers," she explained morosely. "Of course, I will pay for the cup," she offered, but the waiter waved her worries away.

"Don't worry about that. Accidents happen all the time. I will clean the table immediately," the server said. "I'll bring you another cup of coffee afterward," the man promised Ellen.

"I think I'd better pay the bill and leave now," Ellen shook her head.

The woman was already fed up with her clumsiness and how she reacted to Jay's presence. She had turned into an awkward schoolgirl just because the man stared at her with his intense dark eyes.

"No, Ellen," Jay intervened immediately, a pang of anxiety piercing his heart. "Just have another cup of coffee with me," he stopped her, unwilling to see her standing and leaving out of his life once more.

"And you haven't had your brunch yet, miss," the waiter pointed out. "I'll bring it out in a couple of minutes," he promised to her. "You won't have to wait for long."

"But, but..." she started to stammer in agitation, but then Jay laid his hand over hers and stopped her stuttering.

"Stop fretting, Ellen. Sit back and relax. The man will bring us our brunch soon, and we can talk then," Jay said, and his eyes levelled steadily on hers as if he challenged her to dare and refute his invitation.

Ellen didn't reply. She pressed her lips together and drew her hand back from under Jay's fingers. The woman folded her hands in her lap in resignation and allowed the server to clean the table.

Still, Ellen kept her eyes on Jay, wondering what his game was. A little over two weeks ago, the man had practically thrown her out of his apartment. Now, he wanted her to stay. He was more changeable than the wind.

The woman wanted to talk to him but didn't know what subject of discussion he had in mind. She doubted that their intentions were similar.

Jay laid back in his chair, his hands braced on his thighs. He didn't take his eyes off Ellen's face, not even for one moment.

When the server finished his ministrations and left them alone, Jay leaned forward and joined his hands on the table.

"So, let's get back to my previous question," he grinned, knowing that Ellen wouldn't like his approach. "How have you been?"

The woman licked her lips and merely shrugged with indifference. Still, she brushed her hair behind her ears with nervous fingers. Jay's pointed look made her feel self-aware. She hated that she had to remain in front of him in her spotted chemise. She felt as if one of her defence walls had crumbled to her feet.

Jay lifted an eyebrow, nudging Ellen to say something.

"I've been fine," she finally replied with a pout. "What did you think? That I'd lock myself in the house and cry my eyes out because you threw me out of your apartment?" she said peevishly, and her eyes sparkled with repressed resentment.

"Nah," Jay said with a wave of his fingers. "You don't look like the type who would brood."

Ellen tilted her head and inquired with curiosity, "And how do you think I look like?" She regretted her question immediately. Ellen half expected that he would say something mean, and she wasn't disappointed.

"Like you'd have gone out and checked me some more. Although I don't know what bodies you think that I keep in my closet," Jay replied in a challenging tone of voice.

"I was sure you wouldn't be able not to take a shot at me," she replied in a voice filled with bitterness. "I haven't even thought of you," she lied to Jay, looking straight into his eyes.

Jay laughed and shook his head. "You're good at lying. I'll give you that. But next time, if you want me to believe you, don't try to stare me down," he advised her with disdain.

"I'm a police officer. I know how to lie convincingly," she retorted in a miff.

"Maybe most police officers know how to lie," he corrected her with a shrug. "Definitely, the one who told you that you are a convincing liar is accomplished himself. You didn't even realize that he wasn't telling you the truth," he grinned at her.

She clenched her fists in her lap and bit her tongue to stop a curse, ready to roll out of her mouth. Jay just bobbed his eyebrows to her and laughed.

"You just want to upset me," she concluded, tilting her head with curiosity.

The man nodded. "I like seeing your reactions," he confessed. "I hate it when you are cold and standoffish," he explained.

"I'm not cold," she refuted his words, and her brows bunched over her eyes.

"Interesting that you don't deny that you aren't approachable," Jay noted in a meaningful tone of voice.

Ellen just shrugged with indifference. She knew that she kept people at bay. It wasn't worth the effort to allow someone to get too close. They inadvertently hurt her. She remembered that Jay had done precisely that, and not long ago.

"Why is that?" the man asked her, leaning a bit further over the table.

"What?" she pretended not to understand his words.

"Come on, you know what I'm talking about," he waved his fingers toward her.

"Ah, I know what you're asking now," she pretended to have just caught his meaning, and Jay laughed, shaking his head to let her understand that she couldn't fool him.

Ellen grimaced and shifted her eyes toward the lake for a few moments. She gathered her thoughts, and then she looked back at him.

"I don't really like to discuss this subject," she decided to say. "But what the heck, if you insist... People invariably hurt each other. It's just better not to allow anyone to get too close to you," she explained morosely.

"Who hurt you, Ellen?" Jay asked, unwilling to drop the subject. His curiosity about the woman just increased a little more.

The woman shrugged once more and then said, "You, for instance," she replied in a firm tone of voice.

"When I asked you to leave," Jay surmised.

Ellen nodded, although a bit unsure that it was a good idea to reveal that he had the power to hurt her.

"I was hurt and in pain," the man replied dryly. "And you didn't do anything else but judge me based on the fact that you saw me playing cards," he specified.

"Repeatedly," she pointed out.

"All right, repeatedly," he accepted. "But that doesn't define me entirely, does it now? Do you know at least what else I do?" he asked Ellen, and his brows hiked up his forehead.

The man didn't have any illusions. If the woman had been bent in checking him out, he expected that she had rummaged through his house to see what else she could find. And he wasn't the person to lock the doors to keep the people out of his business. He didn't even bother to bolt his studio.

"Not really," she admitted. "I found out your name, your address, and that you had a large family. That was everything. I couldn't find out if you had a job or..." she opened her arms.

"Come on, you must have searched my apartment while I was prostrated on that damn sofa," Jay contradicted her with a set jaw. He disliked being taken for a sucker.

"I thought of that," she confessed with a curt nod.

"And?" he inquired in a tone of voice that showed that he wouldn't have believed her if she had denied that she searched his house.

"I couldn't do it," she shook her head. "It seemed... I don't know," she repeated in a firmer tone of voice. "I just couldn't do it. I saw only your living room, bathroom, and kitchen. I didn't go into your bedrooms," Ellen informed him.

"Bedrooms?" Jay frowned.

"You have three other rooms, don't you?" Ellen affirmed with uncertainty. "The doors seemed to lead to other rooms. They couldn't have been closets," she shook her head. "The doors to the closets looked different."

"You're right. Those are rooms, but only two are bedrooms," the man pointed out.

"Oh, but the den is in the corner of your living room," she noted with confusion.

"And your point is?" Jay tilted his head with an amused grin at the corner of his mouth.

Ellen looked at him, baffled for a few seconds and then fluttered her hand. "It doesn't really matter," she said softly.

Jay shook his head stubbornly and replied with irony, "I doubt it doesn't matter for a police officer like yourself."

"Well, as a matter of fact...." Ellen blushed and started to say something but stopped when she noticed that the waiter was coming with their orders.

"What, Ellen?" Jay raised his left eyebrow inquiringly.

"Our orders are here," she warned him and leaned back to let the server put the food onto the table.

CHAPTER EIGHT

"As a matter of fact, what, Ellen?" Jay asked with stubbornness after the waiter left their table.

Ellen raised her confused eyes at him, and Jay fluttered his fingers with impatience.

"Don't think that I forgot that you were about to say something just before our orders arrived," he said in a warning tone of voice, unwilling to let her off the hook. "I might have been hit over the head two weeks ago, but my memory is still in good functioning order," he thought to mention.

"It wasn't a big deal," Ellen shrugged. She seemed to have changed her mind and didn't want to share that specific fact with him anymore.

"Huh, huh, it doesn't work that way," Jay replied with a shake of his head and reached out to his coffee cup. "You opened this can of worms, so now, you have to spill everything," he said and sipped from his cup afterward, watching her over the rim of the dish.

"I could very well shut the lid back if I want to," she retorted grumpily.

"Not after you incited my interest," Jay shook his head once more. "You don't want me to die and fall over your brunch because you won't satisfy my curiosity," he said in a near whisper. His eyes shifted left and right comically as if he hadn't wanted anyone else to hear what he was saying.

"Far from me to wish that. Of course, I don't want to see you wither and die because you can't refrain your nosiness," Ellen laughed.

But then, she became serious and picked up her coffee cup. She sipped from the hot liquid pensively, and the fingers of her other hand clenched over a napkin.

Jay understood that what she had to say was something that bothered her, and his fingers covered Ellen's to help her relax.

"What is it, Elle?" he inquired softly. "What happened?"

The woman lifted her eyes at him nonplussed, hearing his appellative for her.

"Elle suits you better," Jay shrugged. "You're Elle for me." 'At least, that's how I thought of you,' he continued in his mind.

"No one has called me Elle before," she said.

"That's good," Jay nodded. "You'll be Elle just for me," he decided.

The intensity in the man's dark pupils practically took her breath away. Her fingers quivered under Jay's hand.

The man shook his head to clear it and took his hand off hers. Jay sipped his coffee again to give her the time to pull herself together, but he still observed her.

"I resigned from my position as a police officer," Ellen said and lifted her eyes at him.

"When?" Jay frowned, her confession shocking him. She didn't seem the type of woman who would give up on her work at a whim.

"On Monday, after I brought you home," she revealed with a shrug.

"Why?" the man inquired, his voice filled with bewilderment.

"I didn't feel like I could achieve much in that position," she replied dryly and picked up her fork to attack her eggs, bacon, fries, and salad.

"What do you want to do, Elle?" Jay asked and started eating his brunch as well. But then, his eyes didn't leave the woman's face for more than a second or two.

"I want to prove that the owner of that casino where you were beaten doesn't run an honest business," she turned her eyes at him.

Jay shrugged and said after he swallowed, "No casino owner has a hundred percent honest business," he pointed out carelessly.

"Maybe," Ellen conceded. "But I want to prove that this one organizes games intending to fleece certain people," she continued in a challenging tone of voice.

"That I can assure you that it is true," Jay replied. "That's what he intended on doing to me that night when they beat me. The problem is that I can't be cheated," he added and stuffed his mouth with a piece of bacon.

Ellen looked at him with perplexity. She even shook her head, convinced that she hadn't heard him correctly. "What do you want to say?" she decided to ask.

Jay shoved some eggs into his mouth to gain some time. *'You really needed to open your big mouth,'* he scolded himself. Now, he had to come up with something because Ellen wasn't the woman to let go without probing some more.

"I know you're trying to weave a plausible story, Jay," she warned him. "Can't you just tell me the truth?"

He shook his head, and Ellen frowned. She didn't really expect him to tell her the truth, but she didn't think he would be so frank about it.

"Let's say that I sense if someone wants to cheat me and leave it at that," Jay decided to say.

"Huh!" Ellen scoffed. "I heard others talking about the instinct one needs while playing cards, but from what I could see, it is nothing but a big pile of... rubbish," she edited her words, and Jay grinned.

"You don't need to measure your words with me," he said in a near whisper, leaning forward. "I'm not a shrinking violet, you know," he winked at her.

"Don't change the subject," Ellen replied in a stern tone of voice, laying her fork and knife on the plate, suddenly not feeling like eating anymore.

"I'm not," Jay shrugged. "The problem is that you wouldn't believe the truth even if I wanted or could share it with you. So, we'd better leave it at instinct. Your problem is different, though," he pointed out. "You can't really prove that the owner of that casino organizes those games."

"But I have to," she countered forcefully.

"Why?" Jay lifted an eyebrow quizzically. "And by the way, I don't mind if you continue eating while you explain that to me," he pointed with his fork toward her plate and then used it to shove some more food into his mouth.

Ellen blushed slightly and fluttered her fingers afterward. "I'm not hungry," she replied.

"Of course, you are," the man retorted. "You wouldn't have ordered the pick-me-up menu if you hadn't been."

"Well, I was then," she huffed. "I'm not anymore," Ellen said pointedly.

"I don't believe that," Jay contradicted her, shaking his head emphatically.

"Oh, for God's sake, will you forget about my food?" the woman snapped at him.

"I can't," Jay admitted. "I can't believe that you're filled with only three bites," the man shook his head.

"Don't tell me that you counted how many times I lifted the fork to my mouth," she looked at him askance.

"Believe it," the man nodded. "Everything you do has my undivided attention, Elle," he confessed. "Now, be a good girl and continue eating. Of course, you can also explain why it is so important that you prove that the owner organizes those games. You can do it between bites," he advised her in a tone of voice better used to impart the secrets of the universe.

Ellen grimaced. Jay was worse than a terrier with a bone stuck in his teeth. The light in his eyes didn't leave room for negotiation. The woman stabbed a piece of bacon nervously and stuffed it into her mouth so that he stopped nagging her.

"Satisfied?" she asked after she chewed it furiously.

"I'm far from satisfied," Jay replied. "You have to work a little more for that," he added with a grin, and her eyes thundered at him with annoyance.

Unimpressed, the man waved his hand to her to continue eating, and then he made short work of the food on his plate. Then, he picked up his cup and drank his coffee as well. He didn't push her to talk anymore and didn't say anything before he finished polishing everything.

Jay replaced the cup on the table and leaned back in his chair. For the first time, he took his eyes from her tiny hands and glanced at the lake, breathing deeply.

'Damn, I really missed this,' he sighed inwardly.

Then, the man looked back at Ellen. The woman maneuvered the cutlery with nervous gestures, and a slight grin appeared in the corner of his mouth.

"What do you think about some waffles?" he asked Ellen.

Her eyebrows shot up her forehead, and her fork froze midway to her mouth. "Do you really think I could also eat waffles?" she inquired nonplussed.

He shrugged with nonchalance, "Why not?"

"Sorry, big guy, but I'm not a bottomless pit," she shook her head. "You're unbelievable," she mumbled.

Ellen shoved the fork into her mouth and then placed it onto her plate with care. When she swallowed, she sighed deeply and confessed, "I truly can't have another bite."

"You eat too little," Jay shook his head. "That's why you are so thin."

She frowned at him, ready to give him a harsh reply, but he put up his hand. "I didn't say I didn't like what I saw," he reassured Ellen.

"I don't care whether you liked how I looked or not," she snapped at Jay, and her mouth became a thin line.

The man just grinned and shook his head. "You care, all right," he guessed. "But, as I said, I do like how you look."

"Look here," she started to say with a frown and tapped the tip of her finger on the top of the table.

However, Jay leaned toward her and took her fingers between his hands, stopping her gesture. Now, the woman looked at him nonplussed.

"Don't get miffed with me, little girl," the man whispered with a grin. "You're just fine the way you are, and you know it. Now, if you don't want us that we order those waffles, what are you saying about settling the bill and going for a walk along the shore and then into the Music Garden?" he proposed. "Of course, if you don't have other big plans for the day," he amended his words.

Ellen shook her head. "I don't have any plans for today. As a matter of fact, I don't have any plans for the near future," she confessed morosely.

"That's another thing you have to tell me about," Jay noted meaningfully and turned around to look for the waiter so that he could pay the bill.

Ellen just slid her hand from his and leaned back in her chair. The man had the effect of a tornado on her system. She needed to clear her head.

CHAPTER NINE

Jay grabbed Ellen's hand in his with determination, and despite the woman's attempts to shake his hand off, he didn't let go. He led Ellen purposefully toward the promenade, avoiding other couples or groups of people artfully.

Ellen stole a glance at him without changing her expression. The man didn't seem impressed with the rigid set of her mouth, and she felt like screaming.

Jay didn't doubt that the woman was mad at him and avoided looking at her. He had overridden her and asked the waiter to bring only one bill he had paid in full. He had turned a deaf ear to her protests and overlooked the frown on her face, although it had promised dire retribution.

'She'll get over it, sooner or later,' Jay shrugged inwardly, glancing at her sideways.

He guided her through the thick stream of people and decided to let her stew for a few minutes. He hoped she would cool down soon so that they could talk because he needed a few answers.

Anyway, Jay didn't have any intention of letting her disappear into the crowd. He wouldn't have known where to look for her afterward. Even his idea of looking for Ellen at the police stations was out of the question now.

The man kept the woman close to him and strode leisurely with the step of a man who had enough time to waste. Jay hadn't felt so good in days.

People and sounds surrounded him from everywhere, and the lake glimmered. The soft wind ruffled Jay's hair, and he always loved that. But then, besides that, now, he also held Ellen's elegant fingers in his hand, and he had often thought of that lately.

'She's good for my mood,' he concluded with puzzlement. *'Who would have thought?'*

"You shouldn't have done that," Ellen suddenly said, and her fingers flexed in his palm.

"What?" Jay asked her. He turned his gaze to her, and a crooked smile tugged at the corners of his mouth. He was glad that the woman's words stopped him from analyzing his feelings in depth.

"You know what I am talking about," she replied peevishly, frowning at him.

Indeed, Jay knew what she was talking about, but then, he needed a bit of fun. That day, Ellen's reactions made up for the entire period of boredom Jay had gone through since he took the beating.

"You shouldn't have paid my bill. I can afford to pay for my food," Ellen snapped at him.

"Elle, Elle, Elle," Jay shook his head with fake disappointment. "You missed my point. I didn't pay the bill because I thought you didn't afford it, although you just told me that you didn't have a job anymore," the man pointed out, drawling his words.

Ellen's eyes narrowed in response to his reply, and he grinned with satisfaction. He loved pressing her buttons. The woman attempted to shake off his hand once more, but his fingers just tightened over hers.

"All right, ferocious kitten," he decided to give her a straight answer. "I didn't pay that bill because I thought you couldn't afford it. That never crossed my mind. I did it because I don't go out with a woman and ask her to pay for her food. That's something uncouth, in my opinion," the man confessed, slightly embarrassed. He knew that many people considered him weird because of that.

Ellen stopped suddenly and brought him to a halt too. She turned to him in a huff. Her eyebrows bunched over her clouded eyes, and the woman thundered him with a bleak look.

"Listen here," she snapped at him. "First of all, I'm not a kitten. Second, we're not on a date. We have just met in the restaurant by chance," she exclaimed, and exasperation tainted her voice.

"That just shows that you don't know how ferocious a tiny kitten can be," Jay replied with nonchalance.

The man enjoyed the position. Her breath teased his chin as he tilted his head forward. Due to their closeness, he also felt the vibrations of her body. He had no doubt that the woman was furious now.

"You definitely are a furious kitten right now," he contradicted her in a playful tone of voice. "And our encounter might not have started as a date, but it turned into one," he took care to point the fact to her.

"No, it didn't," the woman practically stomped her foot, a gesture she regretted immediately. She usually was more composed than that.

"Do you want to bet?" Jay grinned at her mischievously, and she practically growled, making him burst into hearty laughter. "Stop overthinking everything, Elle," he advised her when he finally stopped laughing. "Try to take things as they come. Live a little," he stroked the side of her face, and the woman blushed.

Ellen drew back a step, and his hand fell off with regret. Jay loved the texture of her skin.

"Let's find some privacy in a secluded corner and talk for a while. What are you saying?" the man asked her, raising his eyebrows. "I think the Music Garden is the best place for that."

Ellen nodded with hesitation. She didn't know what to think of Jay's behaviour and was afraid he was only toying with her. Still, when Jay retook her hand and pulled her gently after him, she followed without comment.

'He will show his colours soon,' Ellen reflected, matching the man's stride. 'Then, I will leave, no matter what.'

"Let's take a streetcar, Elle," Jay proposed after fifty yards. "There's no point in walking to the garden. It's too far for a pleasant stroll," he observed.

"You do have a fixation with that garden," she replied. "Don't you think that the garden is also crowded at this time of the day?" she pointed out in a dry tone of voice.

Jay stopped brusquely, and Ellen bumped into him because she hadn't expected that. He looked at her with a quizzical expression on his face, and the woman had the feeling that she wouldn't like what he had to say. She was confident that he would find some fault with her again.

"You're right," Jay said.

That surprised Ellen, and she blinked. She didn't expect that.

"With this weather, the garden must be full. I didn't think of that," the man admitted with a shake of the head. "I don't think that there's a corner around here where we could have some privacy," he remarked, looking around with searching eyes.

"My point exactly," Ellen replied. "Let's call it a day, and we can catch up later," she proposed.

"That doesn't work with me, Elle," Jay shifted his eyes back to her. "There's still a place where we'll certainly enjoy some privacy."

"Where?" she arched an eyebrow haughtily.

"You'll see," he tweaked her nose, and she growled, slapping at his fingers.

"Stop that," Ellen barked at him. "And do you think I'm going anywhere with you if you don't tell me where?"

"A big bad girl like you?" Jay teased her. "You're not afraid of going with me, Elle, are you? I dare you," he challenged her with a sparkle in his eyes.

"Dream on, big boy," she retorted.

But then, she felt something melting inside her whenever he called her Elle. She liked his gruff tone of voice anyway, but the man sounded somewhat different when he uttered that word. Still, she couldn't give in too easy, although he had never scared her.

"Dares haven't worked on me for some time now. I'm an adult, after all," she shrugged.

"And that's your problem, Elle," Jay replied. "You're so busy being an adult that you forget to enjoy yourself. Just go with the flow, sweetie. Not all the time. Just now and then. Let's buy a couple of things first," he proposed, and again, the man took her hand and pulled her after him.

"I'm not a dog on a leash," she huffed in a dry tone of voice.

"That I know," he chuckled.

"Then, stop pulling me around in a whim," she said, matching his lazy stride. "What do you want to buy?"

"You'll see," he answered, and a smile tugged at the corners of his mouth.

"I DON'T KNOW WHY YOU bought all those pastries," Ellen remarked when they left the coffee shop.

When they went inside the shop, she had thought that Jay wanted to stop there and talk. She didn't believe that they would have any privacy. But then, the man headed directly to the counter and ordered everything to go.

"I can't believe that you're still hungry," she shook her head in bewilderment.

"They're for both of us," he explained calmly and grasped her hand again. '*You're surely afraid that she will disappear, man,*' Jay reflected with dismay.

The woman laughed with puzzlement and shook her head once more. "I can't eat anything right now, Jay. I'm not hungry. I'm not joking," she warned him.

"Maybe not right now, but you might be soon. We still have to walk for about ten minutes. Your appetite might return," Jay observed with a shrug.

"You still haven't told me where we're going," she noted.

"You'll see soon enough," he led her through the people in the street.

CHAPTER TEN

"I should have guessed," Ellen said with a shake of her head when they entered the lobby of Jay's building.

"Well, here I can guaranty our privacy," the man replied and showed her to the elevator after he greeted the front desk attendant. "Matt will not come because he's upset with me. He still doesn't leave Nora out of his sight, although she recovered completely, so she won't come either," he shrugged. "Bryan and Becka took the kids to the house on the lake, so we are alone, Elle," the man bobbed his eyebrows to her. "That does put ideas into your mind, doesn't that?" he said with a chuckle.

"You are just a clown, Jay," she noted dryly, and the man's eyes sparkled mischievously.

"Come on, sweetie, don't tell me you haven't had a thought or two about catching me alone," the man said, and his fingers stroked her jaw with a featherlike touch.

Ellen closed her eyes for a second, but then, she made an effort to steel herself against Jay's magnetism and brushed off his hand.

"I don't have to tell you anything," she replied, looking straight into his eyes.

"But you do," Jay pointed out. "That's why we're here, after all. So that you could tell me everything."

"No, we're here because you wanted to talk privately," Ellen retorted. "That doesn't mean that I'll do the talking," she countered his argument.

"Huh, huh," Jay shook his head exactly when the elevator doors opened. "You have a lot to tell me," he said and took her hand when he saw that she wasn't moving. "We have to go out, you know. We can't monopolize the elevator. It's a high-rise building, and people won't be too happy if they have to climb the stairs, believe me. We'd better have our conversation in my apartment," he observed and pulled her after him.

"You're too bossy," Ellen huffed but followed him.

"That's calling the pot black," the man retorted. "You probably forgot how bossy you were the night when I got beaten," he observed, leading the way to his flat.

"That was something else," Ellen pierced him with a black glance, which was utterly lost on Jay. The man just strode along the hallway purposefully without looking at her.

"How was it something else?" he asked, turning toward her when he stopped in front of his apartment door.

"I had to make you walk," she shrugged. "I couldn't coddle you."

"And your attitude toward Matt and Bryan?" he inquired, tilting his head.

Ellen blushed violently, but then she shrugged. "I didn't want anyone to hurt you," she explained in a flat tone of voice.

"I wonder why," Jay said, his eyes searching her face avidly.

"You can keep wondering," Ellen snapped. "Was your intention to have that conversation in the hallway?" she inquired sweetly, tilting her head meaningfully toward the door he didn't unlock.

"Yep, I knew it. You're a laugh a minute," Jay mumbled and unlocked the door. Then he stepped aside, inviting Ellen to enter with a wave of his fingers. "Come in, princess."

At his words, Ellen grimaced. Although she didn't think she would feel at ease in his apartment again, Ellen went in before him. She still remembered the hollowness she had lived through when he asked her to leave the last time she was there, and her heart cringed. Ellen worried that their conversation would end the same way. She didn't know whether she could go through a similar circumstance anew.

"Stop being so apprehensive," Jay told her in a stern tone of voice. "I have no intention of being a jerk again," he added, showing that he had read her thoughts with accuracy, and she turned her face away.

"I'm not," Ellen said defiantly, but she doubted that Jay believed her.

'Why the heck I can't keep my cool with him?' she scolded herself. She hadn't ever behaved like that with anyone before.

"Let's go into the living room," Jay invited her with an inward sigh and placed his hand on the small of her back, nudging her to walk in front of him.

Ellen moved her feet, although she started suspecting that her visit there wasn't a good idea at all. She liked Jay a lot, but they seemed like oil and water.

Jay rolled his eyes behind her. He could practically hear the wheels moving in her mind. The man knew that Ellen was looking for everything negative attached to her presence in his house.

"Take a seat, Elle," he showed to the sofa and then took the bag with pastries to the kitchen. "I'll be only a minute," he said on his way there. "You want some coffee, won't you?" he asked her from behind the island.

"Maybe..." she said undecidedly. "I don't really know," she shook her head.

Jay's chuckle came from the kitchen, and Ellen pressed her lips tight. *'Can you be less stupid?'* she scolded herself.

"I'll make some," Jay decided for her. "It will go great with the pastries, you'll see."

Ellen just shrugged but didn't bother to answer back. Her eyes wandered around the room. Nothing had changed from the day she was there. She stood and moseyed to the balcony.

Leaning onto the jamb of the balcony door, Ellen watched the lake with longing. *'How many years have been since I was out on the lake?'* she wondered. *'Maybe twenty,'* she guessed with a shrug.

She must have been six at the time. Her parents had taken her on a trip to the island. It was one of the few outings they had ever had together. They didn't have the time to spend time with each other, and their child came in the last place.

Jay had stopped in the kitchen doorway and stared at her. The man felt her sadness as if it belonged to him. Her posture told him that she would have liked to be there, out, on the lake.

When Ellen brushed her hair over her shoulder, Jay stepped inside the living room and called her softly.

"Elle, are you all right?"

Startled, she winced, shrugged off her melancholy, and then turned to him. "Of course, I am," she replied in her usual no-nonsense tone of voice.

Jay merely shook his head, suspecting that it wouldn't have been a smart move to let her understand that he knew how she felt.

"I'd like to have our coffee on the balcony," he told Ellen. "But my neighbours are nosy," he whispered impishly. "They are about eighty-something and extremely curious. Don't let their age full you. Their hearing is as sharp as ever," he informed her.

Ellen smiled at him. "We can have our coffee inside, away from open ears," she assured him.

"Great," the man rubbed his hands. "But you still have to wait for a couple of minutes," he warned her. "The coffee maker is still huffing. I do have to buy another one soon," he remarked carelessly, like an afterthought.

The woman waved her hand to show that it didn't matter. She had already made the acquaintance of his coffee maker and knew how temperamental it was.

Jay closed the distance between the two of them. He brushed a lock of hair away off her face and then rubbed it between his fingers.

"So silky," the man whispered and lifted his gaze at hers.

Ellen's eyes widened, staring at his fingers, nonplussed.

"I like your hair," the man shrugged negligently. "It is so... vivid, I'd say," he explained with broad gestures, and she shook her head.

"I thought to show you the rest of the house," Jay informed Ellen, taking her hand.

"That's no need," the woman rushed to say.

"Come on, sweetie, don't tell me you don't die of curiosity to see the rest of the apartment," he arched an eyebrow.

"I'll survive," she replied sardonically.

"No need to just survive," Jay pointed out. "I'm willing to give you the big tour," he waved his hand toward the interior of the apartment. "You've already seen the living room," the man mentioned. "I think that we'll skip the hallway bathroom," he led her past the respective room. "You know it, after all," he shrugged. "This is my bedroom," he whispered to her, tilting his head, thus taking advantage of their proximity to have a whiff at her hair.

The man pushed the door open and invited her inside. Ellen stepped inside shyly. The situation seemed too intimate, and she couldn't guess Jay's game.

Her eyes wandered over the green forest drapes, mirrored in the colour of the counterpane. The expanse of a burnt orange carpet complemented the green of the curtains and the cream of the walls.

"It's beautiful," she said softly.

Jay breathed deeply. For a moment, he had thought she didn't like it because she just looked around without saying anything.

"And here's the en-suite bathroom," he showed her the room whose tiles gave the impression of the waves on the North Sea.

"It looks awesome," Ellen smiled at him. "Who decorated the apartment?" she asked.

"I did it. Entirely," Jay boasted, delighted to see that his décor had her approval. "Let me show you the second bedroom," he pulled her after him, and Ellen laughed.

She had already gotten used to him dragging her here and there.

"What?" Jay turned his eyes to her.

"You," she replied. "You pull me all the time in all directions," she pointed out.

"Sorry," he said, but his voice didn't show any repentance for his behaviour.

"Yeah, you're sorry, all right," Ellen mumbled.

"You catch fast," Jay grinned. "So, this is the second bedroom," he informed her, opening the door to the next room, and then he let Ellen go inside in front of him.

Ellen noticed that the man had done that room in various nuances of brown, from dark chocolate to light caramel. The ambiance was warm and welcoming. She wondered how good of a gambler he was that he could afford such an apartment. Even the location of the flat was exclusive.

Jay showed her the en-suite bathroom, and Ellen marvelled at the minute attention to detail and the harmonization of nuances.

The room gave her the feeling that she had just stepped into a tropical jungle.

"Good job, Jay," the woman lifted her face and beamed at him despite her thoughts. "You do know how to play with colours," she observed.

"Hmm... Well, you should see the third room," Jay mentioned with some hesitation.

Ellen's eyebrows raised on her forehead quizzically. The man hadn't shown any kind of timidity until then, and his new attitude puzzled her.

"What's the matter, Jay?" she inquired. Clearly, he didn't seem at ease with showing that room to her. "If you don't want me to see that room, it isn't a problem," Ellen assured him, although a lot of questions popped into her mind.

"Well, you have just to promise not to say to anyone what you see in there," he asked her in a grave tone of voice. "Few people have ever seen that room," he warned her.

Now, Ellen was anxious to have a look at that third room. She watched Jay reaching to the handle of the door with trepidation.

CHAPTER ELEVEN

J ay finally opened the door, and Ellen found herself in the sunniest room of the apartment. A gossamer white curtain, which didn't prevent the light from flooding the space, covered the farthest wall, made entirely of glass.

A board covered with canvas drew Ellen's attention immediately because it appeared to be the room's focal point. Two working tables, lined with several jars, stuffed with brushes and pencils, and Lord knew what, framed the board.

Ellen turned her inquiring haze toward Jay, but his unreadable eyes revealed nothing.

"Are you a painter or something?" she asked hesitantly.

"Or something," he nodded. "As a matter of fact, I'm a graphic artist. I create comics," he shrugged with nonchalance, but Ellen could see that he felt awkward under her scrutiny.

"I always loved comics," she smiled at him. "I still buy them now and then. Do you only ink them or do everything?"

"I plot the story and draw it from A to Z," he replied.

The tone of his voice made Ellen understand that the man was proud and satisfied with what he was doing, although he worried about what she thought of his work.

"Would you show me?" she asked with eager interest.

"Of course," the man grinned at her, but then, he suddenly sobered, and his eyes widened in horror.

"What's the problem?" she frowned slightly, not understanding his abrupt change of heart.

Jay rubbed his chin thoughtfully, eyeing her speculatively. Then, he scratched the top of his head for a few moments and stared at her some more.

"The suspense is killing me here," Ellen said in a flat tone of voice.

"There's a slight problem," the man admitted, utterly uneasy under her scrutiny.

"Namely?" Ellen tilted her head and pressed her lips together. She just knew that it was something she wouldn't like.

"How should I tell you?" he wondered. "Eh, I think you'd better see for yourself," he shrugged, and his features turned stoic. "Go on, take a look," he invited the woman with a gesture, and his heart cringed, expecting the worst.

Ellen stared at him for a moment, and then she headed to the board with purposeful steps. She looked at the scenes depicted, and her jaw fell. The woman gasped loudly, and Jay prepared mentally for a set down.

"What the heck is that, Jay?" Ellen turned and snapped at him.

"You see, I've been thinking of you and...," he shrugged.

"You've been thinking of me," she repeated nonplussed. "And that's how you saw me," she shouted, pointing to the board.

"Come on, Elle, don't get your hackles up. You look great. You can't deny it," Jay tried to calm her down, putting his hands up.

"And a lot of good does that to me," the woman huffed. "You made me into a lunatic vigilante," she protested, throwing her hands in the air.

"A beautiful and charming vigilante," Jay pointed out with a gesture meant to calm Ellen's fury, but then he failed.

"Yeah, I'm impressed. Especially with the way I'm crashing that poor man's feelings," she scoffed. "That's how you see me?" she inquired in a tired tone of voice, disappointed with his image about her.

"The story needed a bit of drama," Jay explained patiently. "It's not you, after all," he shook his head. "Just your face."

And that trim lithe body of yours,' he continued in his mind. He wasn't stupid and knew that Ellen would have had his head if he had uttered those words.

Ellen gave up arguing with the man and tried to storm past him, but Jay stopped her, putting his hands on her shoulders.

"You've seen just two pages, Elle. Look further. You might like the character. I do like her," he confessed. "She's not only beautiful but also strong. That guy is just an idiot, and believe me, he deserved to have his heart crushed under her heel."

After a bit of tug of war, Jay convinced Ellen to read the rest of the story. He remained behind her, with his hands on her shoulders, holding her close to him and enjoying every second.

"It's not bad," she admitted after a few minutes. "But it's still not me," she looked up at Jay.

His closeness made Ellen shiver, and she tried hard not to let him feel it. As a result, she became tense, and Jay began to massage her shoulders to help her relax.

'It doesn't work, you, idiot,' she reflected. 'It's even worse,' she turned her head and closed her eyes, pretending to look at the comics.

Jay grinned and continued his ministration. He knew what he did to her. But then, he relished to have her practically flush against him and feel the shivers passing through her body, so he pretended not to notice.

"You're good," Ellen admitted, and Jay wondered what she was talking about.

"At what?" he couldn't refrain from asking.

"Your comics," the woman snapped at him and stepped away from the man.

She turned to him, and Jay schooled his features so that she wouldn't see what ideas crossed his mind.

"I think I'm ready for that coffee now," she said in a dry tone of voice.

"Wow, I forgot about it," Jay exclaimed and rushed out of the room. "That stupid machine is old, and if I don't turn it off, it splatters everywhere," his voice came from the hallway, and Ellen shook her head.

She glanced at the comics once more, and a smile perched on her lips. 'No, the guy's not bad at all. Jay's got good skill at drawing, and the story is catchy. Of course, it's got a lot of humour and fine irony. That's entirely Jay,' she shook her head and then followed the man's steps toward the kitchen.

"Is everything all right?" Ellen asked, getting into the kitchen.

Jay was busy tearing paper towels and wiping off the counter. He looked at her with a frown.

"Does it look like it's all right to you?" he asked her peevishly, and she shrugged.

"Just making conversation," Ellen said, watching his shrewd moves. "You have some practice with this cleaning stuff," she observed with no bit of surprise.

"My mother believes in equality between sexes. She didn't have too much success in teaching Matt and me to cook, but she did teach us how to keep a clean house," Jay said. He made a ball out of the used paper and threw it in the recycle bin set underneath the counter.

"Hmm, I wonder what she taught your sister," Ellen said with curiosity in her voice.

"Not cooking, for sure," Jay said, pouring coffee into two cups. "To my mother's deep disappointment, none of us managed to master the culinary arts, at which she is indeed awesome," he added. "But then, Maggie knows how to fix the engine of a car."

"Impressive," Ellen nodded.

"Yeah, especially because mom knows zilch about that," Jay grinned. "But she once remained stuck on a country road because her car engine expired, and she decided that Maggie must learn to fix it," he shrugged. "Would you take the plate with pastry?" he tilted his head toward the plateau he had left on the side of the counter and picked up the coffee cups.

"Sure," Ellen nodded and took it, following Jay into the living room.

"You drink your coffee black, from what I observed," he said, laying the cups on the coffee table.

"You have a good sense of observation," Ellen replied flatly, leaving the plateau on the table as well. She took a seat on the sofa because Jay blocked the way to the armchairs.

Jay merely shrugged and sat next to her. Ellen's eyebrows arched, and she looked pointedly toward the armchairs framing the coffee table.

"Nah, I'd feel better next to you," Jay said with another grin and shifted his position to see her better. "Now, it's time you talked," he noted, picking up his coffee cup and waiting expectantly.

CHAPTER TWELVE

"About what?" Ellen pretended not to understand his meaning.

"You played this game before, Elle, and it didn't work," he admonished her playfully, a grin turning the corners of his mouth up.

Ellen just shook her head stubbornly. "I don't recall," she shrugged.

"I do," Jay replied. "Allow me to enlighten you," he said in a haughty tone of voice and placed the cup of coffee on the table. He needed to give his undivided attention to the woman. "First, you have to explain why you resigned from your position. Second, why did you put me under surveillance? Three, what smart plan you hacked to catch that guy into the act," he counted on his fingers, and Ellen grimaced.

"You don't want much," she grumbled with annoyance.

"Nah, I don't think it is much," Jay chuckled. "We'll get to more serious things later," he warned her.

"Like what?" the woman looked at him sideways, with a frown on her face.

"Just things," the man fluttered his hand. "You'll see when we get there. So?"

"So what?" she arched an eyebrow.

"Come on, Elle, you're not dense. So talk. I know when someone is just playing with me," he warned her, bobbing his eyebrows and making her laugh.

"All right, don't get your pants into a twist," Ellen slapped his thigh, and then her eyes widened, surprised by her gesture.

"I like it, so don't fret about it," Jay waved her embarrassment away. "Feel free to touch me in any way you want," he invited her, and Ellen blushed.

"I don't want to touch you," she replied with a pout.

"Yes, you do," the man countered her in a sober tone of voice. "But you can do it while you're talking," he reminded her and took her hand in his. Then he started playing with her fingers.

"I can't focus and talk when you do this," she tried to draw her hand back.

"Huh, huh," Jay shook his head, denying her wish. "It's mine for the moment."

Ellen stared at him, bewildered. His voice showed that the man was serious, and she didn't know what to think of his attitude.

"Talk, Elle," Jay groused through his tightened teeth, intertwining his fingers with hers and giving a slight tug to her hand.

"Oh, for God's sake, I've already told you why I resigned," she practically shouted, sick of hearing the same thing all the time.

"Not really," Jay pointed out. "There's more to that story," he shook his head. "You didn't just decide that you couldn't achieve your goals in the spur of the moment. Something must have happened," the man said, observing Ellen attentively.

Ellen blushed and turned her eyes downward. The woman still shuddered when she recalled how poorly she had managed that situation. She didn't want to share with Jay the awkward scene that had taken place in the commander's office.

"It can't be so bad, sweetie," Jay tugged at her hand again. "Just spill it out, and you'll see that it's not the end of the world."

"I haven't said it was the end of the world," Ellen lifted her gaze at him peevishly.

"No, but your attitude tells me that," Jay replied in a soft tone of voice, and his thumb stroked her palm.

Ellen felt a tingle and closed her eyes for a second. She breathed deeply. Then she opened her eyes and looked directly into Jay's dark pupils.

"All right. Here it goes. I went to the commander with the proposition to arrest the casino owner for what happened to you. He refused, and I insisted. Then, he said that I seemed too closely invested, and he couldn't rely on my words. That pissed me off big time, so I resigned," the woman said fast, to get over with it sooner. "Are you satisfied now?" she thundered him with clouded eyes.

Ellen expected Jay to scoff at her, but the man just shook his head. He flexed his fingers over hers, and then he leaned forward and touched her face gently with his other hand. The woman's lips parted in surprise, and her eyes widened.

Jay leaned even further and touched her parted lips with his mouth. Ellen felt as if a bolt of light had crossed her body, and she sighed into his mouth.

The man deepened his kiss for a moment more, and then, he drew back just a little, leaving only one inch between their faces. Ellen's agitated breath reached his mouth, and a tender smile curved his lips.

Jay's gaze wandered over the woman's flushed face as if he couldn't have had enough of her. His hand was still curled on the woman's jaw, and his thumb brushed over her lower lip.

Then, his slightly dilated pupils fixed on her greenish-brown eyes. They stared at each other for a few more moments. Ellen's fingers shook in Jay's hand, and the man quieted their movement, clasping them in his hand tighter.

Jay's head got closer to her again, and his lips brushed over hers once more. Then, he deepened his kiss and took her mouth the way he had thought about during the long days when he painfully missed her physical presence next to him.

Now, Ellen curled the fingers of her left hand around his wrist while she slid the other one from Jay's grasp and placed it on the man's chest. When it became too much, she knotted her fingers in his t-shirt and held onto him to keep her balance. The woman didn't have any intention to stop him. She just wanted to feel more of him.

Jay ended their kiss with soft nibbles on her lips, and then he let go of her. He drew back and took her hand in his. The man brought their intertwined fingers to his mouth. His lips brushed over her knuckles, and he squeezed them briefly in his hand. With a last soothing stroke over her hand, he untangled their fingers and reached for his coffee cup.

The man felt that he had overwhelmed her and marvelled that he was so attuned to her emotional state of mind. It wasn't the first time he sensed what she needed and what she felt.

JAY'S SALVATION

Jay knew that his empathic skills were rudimentary at best, and he had never been able to sense more than a momentary flash of emotion in the people around him. But then, Ellen's presence in his life seemed to have sharpened his senses because he had a clear picture of her emotional turmoil. The man didn't need to guess what she felt, but what she thought.

He sipped his coffee pensively, watching Ellen from the corner of his eye. The woman clasped her hands together tightly, and she bit her lower lip, unsure of what she should have said or done.

"Don't fret, Elle," Jay said softly, shifting his eyes to her. "It was meant to be," he explained. "The pull between the two of us is strong, and we'd have got to that sooner or later," he shrugged.

Ellen didn't reply but lifted her gaze at him. She measured him with hungry eyes. *'Too bad he's a gambler,'* she reflected with regret and changed her position on the sofa.

"You regret that you kissed me," Jay noted dryly, disappointed with the emotional waves coming from her.

Ellen shook her head. "No, I don't regret that we shared a kiss," she pointed out. "But you're a gambler, and nothing good would come out from a relationship with you," the woman said with determination. Ellen regretted that she had to utter those words, but she knew she would regret much more afterward if she got involved with him.

"I see," Jay grumbled and stood off the couch.

'Now, he'll throw me out again,' she thought with bitterness, unsure of how she felt about that.

Jay just chuckled and shook his head. "You're fantastic, Elle. I've got no intention to send you packing, girl. I just need a drink right now. It's over one in the afternoon," he remarked, glancing at his watch. "We can have a drink," he shrugged. "What's your poison?" the man asked her.

"I don't know. Maybe whiskey or vodka," the woman answered undecided.

"Let's have a whiskey. I've got a good Scottish one," Jay boasted and rushed to prepare the drinks.

The man handed her one of the Glencairn glasses he held in his hands, and Ellen's eyes widened. "These are original Scottish glasses," she remarked.

"You know your glasses," Jay noted dryly. "I learned from my uncle, Michael. He's a whiskey connoisseur, and he taught me to hold my liqueur," he confessed. "To my mother's dismay, I should say," he mumbled. "I had a field day with her when she discovered. And her brother didn't fare better if you want to know," he winked at her. "You'll also notice that I have no ice. I didn't bother to replace it after you used it on my face," he shrugged.

Then, the man swirled the whiskey, holding the glass tightly in the scoop of his hand to warm the liquid. Then, he raised it toward her, "Cheers, Elle."

Jay took a mouthful and let the alcohol warm his palate. *'I'm not at a tasting after all,'* he shrugged inwardly. He hissed when the potent liquid hit his throat and then turned to Ellen, feeling her eyes on him.

"It's strong stuff, so be careful," he warned her, and she shook her head with smile. But then, she just sipped. She didn't dare to follow his example, and Jay grinned.

JAY'S SALVATION

"Would you tell me what you have against gamblers? Where does this aversion of yours come from?" he inquired pensively, and Ellen's eyes lifted at him.

CHAPTER THIRTEEN

Ellen seemed embarrassed to answer his query. She merely stared at him, undecided about what she should do.

"Come on, Elle, you can tell me," he coaxed her. "As a matter of fact, you have to tell me. I'm invested in this thing," Jay waved his hand between the two of them. "I have the right to know against what I have to fight," he said very matter-of-factly.

Ellen shook her head. "You don't have to fight anything, Jay."

"Oh, yeah, sweetie, I do," he nodded emphatically. "You see, the point is that I'm interested in keeping you with me, so I need to know what I'm supposed to do to make that happen," he explained candidly.

"You're so... unbelievable," Ellen observed with another shake of her head. She couldn't believe the man's insistence and didn't understand his ulterior motives because he must have had some.

"Believe it, Elle, and start talking," Jay waved his hand to her impatiently. The suspense tensed him.

"I don't really like to talk about that," the woman tried to explain, glancing at him from under her lashes.

But then, Jay wouldn't have any of that. He just shook his head and asked her again to tell him everything.

Ellen sipped from her glass, taking her eyes off the man. On the one hand, his attitude bothered her, but on the other, she admitted that maybe if he found out what had happened, he would leave her alone.

"My father was a gambler, Jay," Ellen started to talk. "The worst type of gambler, as a matter of fact," she explained, gesturing agitatedly. "He rarely won anything at the tables, although he thought that he only had a run of bad luck," she shook her head as if she still couldn't understand what was in that man's head. "Anyways, soon enough, we were in so much debt that we didn't even have a piece of bread in the house. For days in a row," she blushed with embarrassment.

Jay took her hand in his, and Ellen's gaze fell on their joined hands. The man's gesture made it easier for her to speak about her childhood days, and she didn't understand why.

She shook her head to clear it and continued, "Father didn't work... No time for that, you see," she said with disdain. "He spent almost all his waking hours in a casino, or God knows where. He played cards or dice."

Ellen turned her gaze toward the balcony. She refused to see the expression in Jay's eyes. The woman knew that she would have hated noticing either his reproof or his pity.

"Mother drank," she continued in a tone of voice more appropriate to tell a story. It was as if she didn't speak about her family at all. "That was her way to cope with my father's gambling addiction. Anyway, by the time I was ten, we were on welfare, and most of the money went on playing cards and buying rum... I can't stand the smell of rum even today," the woman shook her head and closed her eyes.

Jay didn't intervene and waited for her to continue in her own rhythm. He just stroked her palm with his thumb and made a note in his mind not to ever keep rum in the house.

"Anyway, when I turned twelve, my father inherited a little house from an older aunt," she turned her eyes to Jay.

The man shivered when he noticed the ice in her eyes and her remoteness. He just knew that the worst part of her story was about to come.

"He sold the house and cashed the money immediately," Ellen revealed in a flat tone of voice. "Then, he went to the same casino where you were and lost every single penny," she continued in the same impassive voice.

"Father came back home at around two or three in the morning and explained everything that had happened to my mother. He told her that the game had been arranged, and that was why he lost his money. I had never seen such a huge fight between the two of them before, although they fought regularly," Ellen shook her head, and Jay pressed his lips when he noticed the paleness of her face. "They practically broke every dish and piece of furniture in that dreary small studio where we lived... Anyway, that morning, he left for good. I have never seen him or heard from him again," she shook her head. "Mother polished two bottles of rum, one after another. She utterly forgot about me. I waited for two days for her to come back to her senses," Ellen recollected with bitterness now.

The woman still remembered how hungry she had been and how she had rummaged through the house for a piece of bread. *'Of course, there wasn't any,'* Ellen recollected.

"Anyways, when she did wake up, she just glanced at me and told me that I had to go away too," the woman shrugged as if it hadn't been relevant.

'Oh, but it was significant, Elle. Downright heart-wrenching, sweetheart,' Jay reflected, and his heart ached for her.

Her story had stirred his anger, but that last comment brought him on the verge of exploding with fury. The people he would have liked to break their necks weren't in that room after all. He breathed deeply, trying to control his rage.

"What happened then, Elle?" he asked when the woman didn't continue with her confession.

Ellen just shrugged, but Jay tugged at her hand, and she glanced at him.

"Actually, that's the end, Jay. I ended up at the Sacred-Heart orphanage first. I lived there for a little over a year. Then, I was placed in foster care," she recollected. "Until the age of eighteen, I met four foster families. It wasn't a big deal," the woman shrugged once more when she saw the flat light in Jay's eyes.

'Yeah, sweetie, I bet it wasn't,' the man reflected with sadness, and then he brought her hand to his lips again. 'You have to think heard, Jay, to come up with a plan to make her stay,' he sighed while watching the woman's profile. He had his work cut out for him.

Ellen drew her hand from the man's fingers and picked up her tumbler of whiskey. The woman busied herself swirling the liquid in the glass because she didn't want to see if he pitied her.

"All right, here's the deal," Jay said in a very matter-of-fact tone of voice.

CHAPTER FOURTEEN

"There's a distinction between a man who gambles to make money and one that gambles for fun," Jay pointed out, watching her expectantly.

When he noticed that her expression hadn't softened at all, the man sighed and stood up, starting to pace the length of the floor. Jay covered the same distance a couple of times, and then, he locked his hands at the back of his head and stopped before the open balcony door.

For a few minutes, Jay just turned various variants in his mind, but he rejected every single one with a shake of his head. By now, Ellen watched his actions with bewilderment. The woman didn't understand what had happened to him.

Suddenly, Jay rubbed his hands and then returned to Ellen. This time, he sat on an armchair so that he could look straight into her eyes.

"All right, the truth," the man sighed. "As a matter of fact, I've already told you the truth, but you didn't believe me," he pointed out. Ellen arched an eyebrow, so Jay hurried to speak. "I did tell you the truth, only not everything. I'm afraid that you won't believe what I am going to say now, either," he took care to mention, leaning forward and bracing his elbows on his knees. "You have to promise something to me, though," he asked, piercing her with his eyes.

"I can't promise anything without knowing what you're asking," Ellen retorted, looking at him askance.

Jay chuckled, but then the woman realized that the man was somewhat anxious, which confused her. He always seemed in control of everything.

"Of course, I won't ask you to make a promise without telling you what's about," he shook his head. "I need your promise that what I'm going to say will stay just between the two of us. No one must know that you found out. Not my brother, not Nora or Becka, and not even Bryan," he pointed out.

"Imagine that I won't start shouting your words from the rooftops," Ellen replied, miffed. "I don't have such a big mouth."

"I haven't said that you do, but maybe, inadvertently, you might say something, and it is important that you don't," Jay warned her. "I'm breaking the rules here and big time, believe me," he stressed out.

"All right, I got that. I promise. Are you satisfied now?" the woman asked in a cross tone of voice.

Jay nodded but didn't seem convinced that things would remain between them.

"Anyway," he started to say with a sigh. "You see, besides my talent with a brush or a pencil, I have another gift. Unfortunately, it isn't a refined gift because of a damned curse," he blurted with annoyance.

"Curse?" Ellen intervened. "Come on, Jay," she scoffed. "Don't sell me one of your stories."

"It's not a damned story," he snapped. "I knew you wouldn't believe me, but anyway, I said I would tell you, so I will," he continued in an upset tone of voice. "If you think that you can keep your mouth shut and won't judge me right from the beginning, of course," he fixed his thunderous black eyes on Ellen.

"I won't say a peep. You will see it. Just go on." Ellen mimicked zipping her lips and then put her hands up.

"You're a mean one," Jay shook his head. "Anyways, I won't bore you to tears with my entire family's saga," he waved his hand. "Suffice to say that I have some empathic skills and some ESP gifts. They're mostly useless because of that dang curse I told you about, but what I can do well, without any failure so far, it is to see the cards," he said with pride in his voice, and that did stun Ellen.

"What do you mean?" the woman narrowed her eyes with suspicion.

"See, you can't keep your mouth shut. Anyways, it's simple," Jay huffed. "I see the cards people hold in their hands. I don't have to rely on luck or counting cards. I don't play for the money. I make enough with my comics," he shrugged.

"Then why are you doing it?" Ellen asked, confused. She still didn't believe him, but at the same time, she wanted to understand what his purpose was to tell her such a weird story.

"It's the only gift I can control, don't you get it? And I need to have the proof that I'm not a complete failure," he admitted ruefully.

"Failure at what? You're talking in circles, Jay," Ellen frowned at him.

The man sighed deeply and brushed his fingers through his hair. It was harder to explain to her than he had expected.

'Matt had it easy,' he reflected, remembering that Nora had to accept everything as genuine when she witnessed what his family could do.

"Let's have some more whiskey," Jay proposed, but then he glanced at Ellen. "All right, I'll make more coffee," he amended his words when he noticed that the woman's eyebrows hiked up her forehead. "By the way, for your information, if someone drinks now and then, he won't turn into an alcoholic," he pointed out, guessing what crossed Ellen's mind. "Even if he gets drunk like a pope."

"I didn't say anything," Ellen blushed under his pointed look.

"But you thought," he retorted and headed to the kitchen, turning his back to her.

Ellen remained on the sofa for a few more moments, and then she jumped up and followed him.

"I don't need more coffee, Jay," she said when she got near him.

"But I do," he said curtly. "I need to drink something, and I can't drink that damn whiskey because you'll think that I'd lose my marbles," he explained at length in a nasty tone of voice. At the same time, he measured water and coffee and then turned the coffee maker on.

"That's plain mean," she observed in a defensive tone of voice.

"But true," Jay retorted.

"I didn't say anything of the kind. You can drink whiskey if you want. I know that people don't become alcoholics if they drink now and then. I am not so retarded," she shook her head angrily.

"Don't put words into my mouth, Elle," Jay groused. "I understand why you react this way, so don't worry. I'm flexible. We can work together," the man added, imploring her with his eyes.

"On what?" the woman looked at him with puzzlement.

"Come on, sweetie. What do you think I am talking about?" he raised his eyebrows. "Or you prefer that I showed you?" he inquired, and a mischievous grin appeared on his face.

"No need for that," Ellen blushed and stepped back. "You'd better explain to me that failure thing," she waved her hand and tried to change the subject.

"Not very subtle, Elle," Jay chuckled.

"Nonetheless, explain," she barked at him, miffed.

"It's not very difficult, from my point of view. Now, the difficult part is that you won't believe me," Jay shrugged.

"Just try," Ellen said through her teeth, tired of Jay's prevarication.

"I was born with some skills, like everyone in my family," he tried to explain to her patiently once more. "Not everyone has got the same skills," he pointed out. "For instance, Matt can read your mind," Jay said.

Ellen arched her brows, and Jay scowled.

"I know what you think, but he can if he wants to, of course. Because he has reached the point where he can control this gift," the man said. "I was supposed to read people's emotions and to sense their actions, among other things," he shrugged.

"Honestly, up to now, with you, I haven't succeeded in reading emotions very well. Anyway, I can see the cards someone has in his hand. I can also read the words on the back of a piece of paper or carton. This is the only thing I can control," he pointed out.

"Why?" Ellen asked in a matter-of-fact tone of voice. "Not that I believe this story," she warned him. "It's too phantasmagoric for my taste," she rolled her eyes.

"Yep, I knew that you'll react like this," Jay shook his head. "Anyway, all of us are under a curse," he said with a sneer.

"That's what I want to hear about," Ellen said with irony and propped her hip on the counter.

Jay tweaked the woman's nose and said, "You can laugh at me if you want to, but it is not so easy for any of us. I'm talking about my cousins and me," he specified. "Becka and Matt have already broken the curse."

"Out with that curse," Ellen nudged him with a finger in his ribs.

"Easy, love," Jay drew back. "I'm not a hundred percent well," he warned her.

"Oh, sorry, I forgot. Did it hurt?" the woman asked solicitously and placed her small hand on the spot she had pocked.

"Nah, you didn't push too hard," Jay brushed his fingers through her hair.

JAY'S SALVATION

"So, the curse then?" Ellen insisted, and the man laughed.

"I'll tell you, just be patient. So, my great-grandmother put a curse on all of us," Jay said.

CHAPTER FIFTEEN

"Why the heck?" Ellen's eyes widened. "Doesn't she like you?"

"She does, in her own special way," Jay grimaced. "By the way, when you meet her, don't pay attention to anything she says or does," he took care to caution her.

"I doubt that I will meet her, so the point is moot," Ellen shrugged.

"Not so moot, Elle," Jay shook his head.

The man slid his arm around her waist and brought the woman closer to his body.

"If I have my way, you'll meet everybody," Jay whispered. "Oh, gosh, you'll have not to pay attention to what the others are saying either," the man grimaced. He remembered his stunt with Camilla. He expected that everyone would pull his leg again and tell Ellen everything.

"Interesting," Ellen lifted her eyes at his face. "That means that I shouldn't pay attention to anyone in your family."

"Yep, pretty much that's what it means," Jay nodded.

"I wonder why," she narrowed her eyes and watched him speculatively.

"That's a story for another day," he shook his head and drew her closer.

Now, their bodies touched, and with a wolfish smile, Jay leaned down to steal another kiss from her. That very moment, the hiss of the coffee maker filled the kitchen, and the man let go of Ellen, swearing.

"The dang coffee maker," he mumbled and rushed to turn it off.

Ellen laughed, and Jay turned his head toward her. "You're having fun on my expenses," he growled, but the lights in his eyes told Ellen that he just joked with her.

"Yep, big guy, I am," she replied mischievously.

"You know that I'll have to punish you for that," Jay replied playfully, taking care of the coffee maker at the same time.

"You can dream on," the woman retorted.

"You should know that I always dream, Elle," he advised her. "And I always find a way to fulfill my dreams," he bobbed his eyebrows to her.

"Yeah, sure," she waved her hand negligently.

"You'll see," he warned her. "Surely, don't you want some coffee?"

Ellen shook her head. "Only if you want to take me to the emergency room afterward."

"I'd rather take you somewhere else," the man replied with double-entendre and looked at her expectantly.

"Aha, keep dreaming," she lifted her chin with obstinacy, waving her fingers, and Jay chuckled.

"All right, let's go back to the living room," he stretched his arm to her, and she took his hand, although she found it foolish to hold hands inside the house.

"The curse?" she reminded him.

"Keep your curiosity in check. We'll get to that darn curse in a minute," Jay said, helping Ellen sit on the sofa.

Then, he remained standing, his eyes going from the armchair to the spot next to Ellen.

"Just decide, for God's sake," she exploded when she couldn't take his indecision anymore.

"I'd love to sit next to you, but that won't help with my telling about the curse. You're too tempting," the man confessed.

"Then sit in the armchair," she huffed. But then she felt a strange satisfaction bubbling in her chest because of Jay's words.

"All right," Jay said and sat down in the armchair closer to her. "What I'm going to tell you will make your eyes definitely cross," he said afterward.

"Try me. I'm not so weak," Ellen shrugged.

A grimace appeared in the corners of Jay's mouth. He knew better what he was talking about.

"Anyways, here it goes," he breathed deeply. "My grand-grandmother is a witch."

"Huh!" Ellen exclaimed and looked at him with wide eyes. "Are you all right? Have you checked your concussions?"

"Yeah, I am all right," he waved his hand. "But you do need to keep an open mind for what I have to tell you. I imagine that it sounds outlandish for regular people," he shrugged. "I grew up with that, and I don't find anything out of the ordinary."

"But a witch, Jay? Like in that one with a magic wand?" Ellen asked, and her eyes rounded in disbelief.

"Nah, that's for kids. Grandma doesn't need a magic wand. She merely needs focus."

"What the heck are you talking about?" Ellen lost her patience.

"I could show you. Or at least, I could try to show you," Jay said with a shrug. "I've never been too good at the magic stuff. I prefer other things," he explained. "Not that I'm good at them either," the man mentioned with bitterness.

"How would you show me?" Ellen asked with suspicion in her voice.

"For instance, tell me what you'd want me to create for you from thin air. Not a horse, please. The spell might succeed, although I doubt it. But then, I'll have a hard time explaining a horse in the apartment. I won't be able to make it disappear for sure. As I've already said, I'm not very good at this stuff," Jay chuckled, but Ellen observed that he wasn't at ease.

"So, I could ask for something, and you will try to produce it from thin air," she looked for clarification, leaning forward, her curiosity pricked.

"Yep. Oh, I forgot to tell you. No jewelry or anything similar. That's a sacred rule that I can't break. We can't obtain material gain with our spells."

"Interesting," the woman murmured. "All right, something that won't cause you any trouble. Let me think," she put up her hand. After a couple of seconds, she said, "I know what. I'd like a bowl with pistachio ice cream, topped with whipped cream and chocolate topping," she decided, smiling like a cat.

"I knew you were a kitten, Elle," Jay shook his head and then closed his eyes. "You couldn't have chosen a small ball or an apple," he grumbled with annoyance.

Ellen watched him a minute attentively, and her brows shot up on her forehead. Drops of sweat appeared on the man's temples, and his lips tightened in a thin line. Suddenly, he waved his fingers toward the coffee table, and a bowl of ice cream appeared. Ellen cried out, and her hand flew at her chest.

"Oh, my God," she murmured. "I can't believe it."

"Believe it," Jay opened his eyes and said in a tired tone of voice. "It wasn't easy, mind you," he added.

"And you didn't get the flavour either," Ellen burst into laughter after she had leaned over the bowl to check it. Three large cherries topped the whipped cream and ice cream.

"Oh, damn," Jay leaned over the table too so that he could have a better view. "I told you that I am not good at that," he waved his hand with disdain. "Thank God, you didn't order a dog. We might have gotten a tiger or something," he shook his head and chuckled. "You know, that happened to Maggie once. She asked for a tiny kitten, and we found ourselves sharing the house with a huge panther. We were about ten at the time," he remembered with a smile on his lips. "Mother wasn't at home to take care of the problem. We couldn't call the animal services, imagine. Father managed to lock us all in his study until mom returned. She made the panther disappear. The housekeeper was on the verge of hysteria," he chuckled at the memory.

"Your mother? Why didn't your father take care of the panther?" Ellen looked at him, askance.

"Father's not a witch. He's just a regular person like you," Jay informed her.

"Oh, I see," she murmured and absently started eating the ice cream. "Not bad," she nodded toward Jay.

"You've got guts to eat that," he shook his head as if he couldn't have believed it. "I wouldn't dare to eat something I created so that you know."

Ellen just waved the man's words away. "It's great. It's not pistachio, that's true," she didn't forget to poke at him.

Jay just shrugged. "I told you I'm no good at that. Now, do you believe me?" he asked, and expectation glimmered in his eyes.

"In a way," the woman admitted. "In an abstract way. I don't actually want to process this side of yours. Anyway, you still have to tell me about the curse," she pointed her spoon at him.

"I forgot," Jay shrugged. "Anyways, great-grandma is a witch. She was married to a witch, and the man left her for another woman. The worst, he threw a spell on that woman to fall in love with him, which is something that we shouldn't do," the man pointed out.

Ellen just listened to him, captivated. She even forgot to eat her ice cream.

"Then, a couple of years down the road, Evelyne, my great-aunt, her daughter, committed suicide," Jay continued. "She had been left standing at the altar. Another woman, always a witch, had thrown a spell over the groom. That made grandma curse all generations to come," he grimaced. "Like in a bad soap opera," he shook his head.

"Anyways, we can't reach our full powers if we don't accomplish something specific. I'm sorry, I can't tell you about that," Jay shook his head. "I can only assure you that it doesn't include killing someone or taking a princess prisoner in the dungeon," he hurried to say when Ellen frowned. "It's something related to our emotional development if you want," he waved his hand to her.

Ellen tilted her head and observed him through narrowed eyes. "I want you to prove to me that you can read cards," she said, and Jay's eyes widened.

He looked at her baffled for a few seconds and then nodded. "All right," he said. "I always keep a pack or two in the house. Sealed, I mean," the man rushed to say so that she didn't get any wrong idea.

Jay bent and opened one of the drawers of the coffee table and took out a few packs of cards. He discarded two of them. "They're already open," the man explained. "Choose one of the ones that are sealed," he invited her with a gesture.

Ellen chose a pack of cards and lifted her eyes at him. "What now?" she asked.

"Well, let's make it ironclad," Jay replied. "I will turn around. You open the pack and choose five cards. Put them face-down on the table, but not in a pile. It's more difficult that way," he shrugged.

"I'll still be able to tell what cards are on the table, but it will take me a little longer than a few seconds. Anyways, hide the others after you lay the cards. Then, you'll tell me to turn around, and I will guess what cards are on the table," he explained at length.

"All right, turn around," Ellen waved her finger to make him move.

Jay stood and strode to the kitchen, keeping his back at her. When the woman called him back, he found her leaning back on the sofa, and five cards were scattered in front of her on the coffee table.

The man grinned, and his eyes swept over the cards for a few seconds. "So, the first one," he pointed to the card in question. "That's the Queen of clubs. The second is the ten of diamonds," he moved his finger toward the next one in the row. "The third is the four of spades. The fourth is the King of clubs, and the fifth is the Ace of diamonds," he finished and lifted his eyes to Ellen.

The woman watched him, stunned. "Unbelievable," she whispered. "You really can read them."

"That's what I've been telling you for a while," Jay replied dryly.

"Once more," Ellen insisted. She still couldn't believe that the man was able to tell what cards she had laid on the table.

"If you wish," Jay shrugged and returned to the kitchen.

Ellen replaced three cards and took out three new cards from the pack she had hidden behind her. The woman played with their position and changed their row a few times. She sighed and called Jay afterward.

"You can come back."

Jay returned with his hands in his pockets. His eyes perused the cards, and a wolfish grin flourished on his lips. He shook his head and said, "Did you really think you would confuse me if you changed their spot on the table?"

Ellen shrugged but didn't comment. She was, in fact, speechless.

"So, let's see. You have here the ten of diamonds, then the Queen of clubs, the King of clubs, the seven of spades and the four of hearts," Jay indicated every card in the row.

Ellen shook her head. "You are amazing," she stared at him. "This is awesome, Jay."

Jay grinned at her. "I finally managed to make you admire me for something."

"Don't worry, I have admired you for other things as well," she replied with a smile.

Jay dropped on the sofa at once and reached out to Ellen. He pulled the woman in his arms and watched her face intently. Jay lifted his fingers to her lips and brushed her lower lip with his thumb. Then Jay leaned over her to replace his thumb with his mouth.

A knock sounded on the front door, and Jay immediately drew back. He jumped up to his feet and rushed to gather the cards and shove them into the drawer underneath the coffee table.

Ellen watched the man's agitated moves with bewilderment and asked, "What's going on?"

CHAPTER SIXTEEN

"**O**nly my family is allowed to come upstairs without having to go through the front desk. And that only during the day," Jay explained to her. "So, it must be one of them. Remember that I asked you to promise that you wouldn't say a word about what I told you?"

Ellen nodded, watching him with her greenish-brown eyes.

"Well, we're not allowed to reveal the family secret. So, keep quiet, all right?" he implored her with his eyes, and then he went to open the door.

The knock had become insistent and got on his nerves. Jay opened the door with an anxious gesture.

"What the heck...," he started to shout. But when he faced his mother and father, Jay swallowed his words. "Hey, mom, dad. Interesting to see you here," he noticed.

"Stop fooling around, Jay," her mother scolded him. "I found out everything."

"I see," Jay said dryly. "Matt and his big mouth, I suppose," he added.

"You haven't given a sign for over two weeks, son," Jonathan, his father, replied in an apologetic tone of voice.

"We don't have to apologize to him," Marjorie snapped. "He didn't tell us what happened to him and let us fret. And what about that hussy who dared to throw my Matt out of your apartment? Who is she?" his mother continued to thunder.

"Mother," Jay started to say in a warning tone of voice, but Ellen's voice stopped him.

"I'm the hussy," the woman announced in a flat tone of voice, and Jay winced. He hoped that Ellen hadn't heard his mother's words.

"Step aside, son," Jonathan ordered. "I want to see the girl," he nudged Jay to move with a bit of push for encouragement.

He measured Ellen openly and then remarked, "She's a pretty hussy. Good for you, son," he thumped Jay over the shoulder. "Maybe you want to make the introductions, though," the man arched his eyebrow, still smiling at Ellen. She watched the tall, dark man in bewilderment.

"Mother, father, this is Ellen," Jay told his parents. "Elle, this is my mother, Marjorie, whose mouth sometimes runs without thought," he said. His mother pierced him with a pointed look. Jay just smirked and continued with his introductions. "This is my father, Jonathan."

"Elle?" his father inquired with a slight frown of puzzlement. "You told us that her name was Ellen."

"She's Elle just for me," Jay snapped. "You will call her Ellen."

Jonathan chuckled and shook his head. He turned to Marjorie and said, "Your son was always a weird one."

"He's my son when he's weird, huh?" she elbowed her husband in his ribs, and he groaned.

"Have a care with my ribs, love. I'm not a spring chicken anymore."

Marjorie waved her hand to quiet Jonathan and turned to Ellen. "I'm Marjorie," she said.

Ellen blushed, and hesitantly, she reached out to shake hands with Jay's mother, only to find herself embraced warmly by Marjorie. She froze, unable to react.

Jay's mother hugged the young woman and whispered in her ear, "That thing with the hussy was only for Jay. I merely wanted to provoke him so that he had said everything to me. So, don't take it personally."

"What are you saying to her?" Jay pulled Ellen out of Marjorie's arms and drew her to him. The man's brows bunched in a frown, and his jaw was set.

Jonathan shook his head. "This one is worse than Matt," he noticed, and Marjorie agreed with a nod.

"It seems so," she mumbled. "Don't you invite us inside, son?"

Jay's eyes turned in a panic toward the living room. He had forgotten about the ice cream bowl and was afraid that his mother would see it and guess everything. Ellen merely intertwined her fingers with his and squeezed his hand reassuringly.

"What's the problem, son?" Jonathan frowned, sensing that something wasn't right.

"I think that Jay worries because I wanted ice cream, and he ordered only one. He doesn't want to seem impolite because he can't offer you one as well," Ellen explained to them in a calm tone of voice.

'Smart girl,' Jay reflected. 'Why haven't I thought of that?' he mused.

"We don't care about ice cream," Marjorie waved her fingers with nonchalance. "Actually, we brought some food and desserts for you," the woman mentioned, pointing to the large bag that her husband had left near the door.

"Oh, yes," the man hurried to pick up the bag. "I forgot about it," he confessed. "You know, with all this discussion," he shrugged. "Mom brought you a lot of goodies," he informed Jay, handing the bag to him.

"Thanks, mom," Jay said with enthusiasm, and his eyes sparkled greedily. His thoughts had frequently gone to his mother's culinary treats while he was stuck in the house.

Marjorie waved his words away and pushed past Jay the living room. She sat on the couch and invited Ellen to join her with a gesture.

"Come here, dear. Let's talk for a bit. Jay will be busy with the food," she noticed, not without a slight irony. She knew her boy well.

Ellen turned her eyes to Jay, looking for advice, but the man merely shrugged. Jay didn't know what to say.

"My wife won't eat her," Jonathan pointed out and put his arm around Ellen's shoulders, steering her toward the couch. "You can keep us company until Jay takes care of that bag," he said.

Watching them, Jay sighed inwardly. The man didn't exclude the possibility that Ellen would tell them something that she shouldn't. Also, afraid that his parents would say something to upset Ellen, Jay wanted to return to the living room as soon as possible. Then he hurried to the kitchen to take the food out.

Jay started taking various dishes out of the bag and shoved them into the fridge without even looking inside to see what his parents had brought.

"Oh, Jay, you're comical," Ellen's voice came from the door, and he turned to her.

"Why are you saying that?" he asked, holding a glass container in his hand.

"You're too anxious, and you'll make them guess a lot of things," she got closer to him and whispered. "You have to play it cool as if you didn't have any worry in the world," she shook her head. "Anyway, I've come to make some coffee," she mentioned in a normal tone of voice and turned to the coffee maker. "Maybe you want to look inside those dishes. Some might need to go into the freezer," the woman advised Jay, taking the carafe to fill it with water.

Jay's eyes followed her every move. The man had forgotten about the dish he held in his hand and the door of the fridge still open. Ellen's supple steps and the delicate balance of her hips fascinated him.

"Besides, it would be nice to lay something on a plate and serve your parents," she told him while filling the carafe with water.

Ellen had sensed his eyes on her and didn't want to let him understand that she was aware of what he was doing. She felt more and more beautiful under Jay's stares, which boosted her self-confidence. The man was good for her ego.

'And he's not only a handsome guy. He's also interesting, intelligent, and caring. Now, that's a fantastic combination,' she mused. *'I don't think I've ever met someone like him or who made me feel the way he does,'* she shook her head.

"What is it, Ellen?" Jay's voice came from behind her, and then, she realized that the water kept running and spilling over.

"Nothing, just thinking," Ellen replied and turned off the tap.

"Not so fast, sweetie. Something bothers you," Jay blocked her way when she wanted to return to the coffee maker.

"Actually, no," Ellen beamed at him. "I've just ordered some ideas in my mind," she tapped her head with the tip of a finger.

Jay grimaced, thinking of the worst, and Ellen laughed. "Don't worry, Jay. I promise that everything is good," the woman said, putting her hand on his chest. She could feel that the man's heart pulsed faster, and the corners of her mouth turned up.

"That's good," Jay replied in a quiet tone of voice, and leaning forward, he brushed his lips to her mouth.

Then, he stepped back and took the carafe from her hand. "I'll make the coffee," he decided. "You take care of that plateau you were talking about. That's something else I don't know how to do," he grimaced.

"You know plenty," Ellen whispered, and for the first time, she took the initiative and reached to him on tiptoes. She gave him a feather-like kiss, stroking the side of his face at the same time. "I'll take care of the platter, don't worry," she grinned, seeing his baffled eyes.

CHAPTER SEVENTEEN

E llen laid the platter on the coffee table and sat back next to Marjorie, whose dark blue eyes followed her every move. *'Matt's got her eyes,'* Ellen noticed.

Marjorie shifted her eyes to the platter and grinned. "That's something you've done. Jay would have thrown a couple of things there is a sloppy manner. I tried to teach him, but I failed," the woman shook her head with exaggerated sadness, and Ellen laughed.

"Well, he's fine the way he is," the young woman noted, and Jonathan nodded in agreement.

"Matt told us that you saved Jay's hide," he opened the subject he and his wife wanted to discuss.

Ellen shrugged. "I just helped."

"We've heard a different story," Marjorie frowned. "I understand that five guys beat him, and you had to intervene with a gun to stop them."

"As I said before, Matt has a big mouth," Jay said, coming with a tray with coffee cups and putting it onto the table. "This family is unbelievable," he said to Ellen. "If you sneeze in the morning, by noon, every single member of the family has found out."

"We're not talking about a sneeze here, Jay," his father intervened in a stern tone of voice.

Ellen noticed the sparkle of annoyance in Jay's pupils and said, "Jay is fine, and that's what matters."

"If he hadn't been so stubborn and had stopped going to casinos to play cards, nothing like that would have happened," Marjorie remarked dryly.

"But then, I wouldn't have met Ellen," Jay retorted in a huff.

Marjorie measured him carefully and shook her head. "What's meant to happen? It will happen anyway, son. You might not have met her there, but you would have definitely made her acquaintance."

"You can't know that," Jay replied in an angry tone of voice.

"I'm very sorry, but now I'm confused," Ellen interfered, and everybody turned to her. "What's the subject of discussion now?"

Jonathan chuckled. "If I were to guess, Jay's just declared his intentions to keep you."

"I'm not a lost dog," Ellen replied in a dry tone of voice.

"Of course, you aren't, sweetie," Jay waved his father's words away and sat on the armrest next to Ellen. He brushed his lips over her temple and stroked her shoulder.

"I see that you've brought the cups," Marjorie said. "I don't see any coffee or sugar or milk," she added meaningfully.

"What the heck?" Jay practically shouted, upset that he was interrupted.

Ellen squeezed his hand. "Only bring the coffee, Jay. I'll come to help you with the sugar and milk," she pushed him aside so that she could stand.

"No, you stay here. I'll bring everything in a moment," the man stopped Ellen's intention and left for the kitchen again.

Marjorie and Jonathan exchanged a meaningful look. Ellen noticed the exchange and asked, "What's going on?"

"Nothing," Marjorie rushed to say. "We're just happy that our son found you."

"What do you mean?" Ellen asked, confused.

"It is quite simple, young woman," Jonathan intervened. "Jay is hooked. For the first time in his lifetime, he really has feelings for someone. I'm sure you noticed how much he cares for you," the man arched his eyebrows.

Ellen shook her head, rejecting his words.

"What the heck, father? Do you really need to tell her that I love her before I can do it?" Jay snapped from the kitchen door.

CHAPTER EIGHTEEN

Ellen's eyes widened so much that they invaded her entire face. She stared at Jay nonplussed.

"You seem really thrilled with my feelings," the man remarked in a dry tone of voice.

The woman just waved her hand speechless. She wasn't able to utter one word and swallowed hard.

"The suspense is killing me, Elle," Jay groused, filled with anxiety.

"Give me a moment," she snapped at him. "It's not like I hear something like that every day."

Then, Jay understood that she was just stunned and grinned. "All right, sweetie, take your time. I can wait," he reassured her, his anxiety gone now.

"Maybe we'd better go home," Marjorie said to Jonathan. "They probably need to talk alone," she pointed out.

"All right," Jonathan slapped his hands on his knees. "Keep us posted, Jay," he turned to his son, and Jay nodded.

"Let me know if I can organize a party for next Sunday," Marjorie didn't forget to mention.

Jay waved his hand, signalling that he heard her words, but his eyes didn't leave Ellen's face.

"And we'd like to visit with Ellen and get to know her," his mother insisted, but Jay didn't react.

Jonathan just shook his head. "I told you," he said to his wife aside. "He's worse than Matt."

"Ah, by the way," Jay intervened when he heard the name of his brother. "If you see Matt, tell him that I want him to sue the casino owner on my behalf."

Ellen's lips parted, and now she looked like something had hit her over the head. Too many surprises came one after the other.

"Justice will be made," Jay said to her in an undertone.

CHAPTER NINETEEN

"Jay, I am not sure that I understand what's going on through your head," Ellen said to Jay once his parents left. "Plus, you've just sent your parents back home after you put that huge platter on the coffee table," she glanced at the dish, filled with pastries and cakes. It had remained untouched in the middle of the coffee table.

"We can eat everything. It's not a problem," Jay waved his hand impatiently.

The woman laughed nervously. "If you think that I still can eat, you've lost your mind," she shook her head.

"Come on, Elle, it's the afternoon already. I'm sure you can eat something," he said in a persuasive tone of voice, sitting next to her and taking her hand to play with it.

"You're unbelievable," Ellen shook her head, an uncertain smile on her face. "Would you explain what just happened?"

"I thought that I was paying attention," the man replied in a soft voice. "Let's see what you didn't get," he invited her to talk.

"For instance, that part about Matt and suing the casino owner," Ellen frowned.

"Ah, that's easy," Jay lifted her eyes at her with a grin on his lips. Then he sobered and said, "It's the only possibility to have your revenge, Elle. You can't prove that a game is rigged," he shook his head.

Ellen tried to say something, but Jay squeezed her hand. "You can't, Elle. We can prove that the casino owner ordered his men to roughen me up. Matt's a very prudent man, you see. He had already asked me if I wanted to sue. He also took pictures with my bruises if I would change my mind because I refused at the time. With those pictures and your testimony, we can get that guy, and his goons, charged. Of course, to make sure that we didn't leave anything to chance, we'll also sue them in a civil lawsuit," Jay explained his thoughts in detail.

"But you wouldn't like to go through a lawsuit," Ellen pursed her lips.

"You missed my point, sweetie," Jay shook his head. "I didn't want it then. Now, I definitely do, and I promise you that we'll have the man's hide," he looked straight into the woman's eyes with confidence.

"But why have you changed your mind?" Ellen searched Jay's eyes.

"Because you need to have the casino owner indicted," Jay said in a very matter-of-fact tone of voice.

"No, I won't ask you to do something you don't like," the woman shook her head. "I'll find something else."

Jay tugged at her hand, "Elle, listen to me. There's nothing else. And don't worry about my disliking it. As a matter of fact, I like that idea more and more," he reassured her. "Believe it," he groused, annoyed to notice doubt in the woman's eyes.

"That's an unusual change of heart," Ellen remarked.

"Probably, you haven't paid attention to the other part of the discussion," the man replied dryly.

Ellen blushed, a sign that, in fact, she had paid attention. "That part is also unbelievable, Jay," she replied.

"What's so unbelievable?" he frowned.

"Two weeks ago, you asked me to leave because you couldn't stand to look at me anymore. We've met again today, and suddenly, you're... in love," the woman noted with disbelief in her voice. "No one falls in love in a few hours," she pointed out in a sarcastic tone of voice. "You must have something else in mind," she shook her head.

"I haven't asked you to marry me yet," Jay snapped at her. "Anyway, for your information, some people fall in love in less than an hour," he pointed out in a nasty tone of voice.

"Huh!" she scoffed.

"Becka and Bryan did," Jay said.

Ellen looked at him, confused.

"Don't look at me like that. Becka and Bryan did, and the love between them is still growing strong," the man said. "Anyways, that's not here or there. I was fed up with my bruises and your constant judgments when I asked you to leave. That doesn't mean that I didn't like you, even then. I liked you all right. Quite too much," Jay mumbled. "I couldn't take you out of my mind for days. Even today, I decided to go out only because you kept popping into my mind, and I couldn't do anything," he confessed.

"But to tell your parents," Ellen started saying, but Jay interrupted her with an angry shout.

"I haven't told them anything," he dropped her hand. Jay got off the couch, feeling the need to move. He started toward the kitchen, but suddenly, he turned back to her. "They guessed if you haven't noticed," he added before disappearing into the kitchen.

"What are you doing?" Ellen rose, as well, looking after him.

"I don't know," the man admitted. "I just need to move."

Ellen's brows climbed up her forehead, and the woman shook her head, surprised.

"Why?"

"I don't know," Jay's voice came from the kitchen. "I'm just too agitated," he added.

"What's going on, Jay?" Ellen came to him and found him at the window, watching outside.

"I'm upset," he replied without turning to her.

"With me," she surmised.

"With you," he nodded. "And with me."

"You're a strange guy, Jay," she laughed. *'Will I ever understand how his mind works?'* she wondered.

The man shrugged and stretched his hand to her. Ellen hesitated for a second, and then, she got closer to him and put her fingers in his hand timidly.

"Elle," he said, almost inaudible, playing with her fingers and staring at her small hand in his. "Why won't you give me a chance, I wonder?"

"A chance? To do what?"

"I can feel your distrust," Jay shrugged. "You like me, in a way, don't you?"

Ellen laughed nervously and nodded. "I do, and maybe, a little too much."

"Is that so bad?" he lifted his gaze to hers, and lights glimmered in his pupils.

"I don't know," she almost whispered. "I've always avoided any kind of relationship. I don't believe in love or anything of the sort," she confessed.

"I do," he said quietly. "I haven't been in love before now, that's true. But I witnessed my parents' relationship, Elle. I can see how Becka and Bryan are together. What the heck, I had a lot of fun when Matt fell in love," he burst into laughter and shook his head.

"Maybe you haven't had the chance to see how it works. But let's find together," he became serious and fixed his eyes on her face.

The intensity in his black eyes stole the woman's breath away. Ellen licked her lips nervously, and she lowered her eyes. She looked at their joined hands, and a sort of longing pierced her heart. She shook her head, willing it to go away.

Jay tugged at her hand, and Ellen lifted her eyes to his face.

"It's not difficult," he whispered, drawing her to him and sliding his arm around her. "Just go with the flow, little girl," he buried his face in her hair and kissed her temple.

Ellen liked the way Jay's body felt against hers, and she leaned her head on the man's chest. Jay still kept one of her hands in his, so she slid the other around his waist and fit her body to his better. A contented sigh flew off her lips, and Jay grinned.

'I'm getting there. I'll go through all your walls, sweetie,' he promised himself.

Jay held her for a long time, just brushing his lips over her hair and temple. She snuggled against him like a kitten, content with the man's tenderness.

"Let's polish that platter with pastries," Jay proposed after a while.

Ellen lifted her head and watched him in bewilderment. "No, really, are you still capable of eating all those pastries?"

"With your help? Sure," he shrugged.

"Forget about my help, big guy," she drew back from his arms. "I need a few hours more until I can swallow anything else."

"All right, let's just talk, and I'll eat," Jay proposed. "But you'll go out to dinner with me," he decreed.

"Are you thinking of anything else than food?" the woman wondered.

"Sure," he replied, looking straight into her eyes. "It's too soon for that, I'm afraid. But I've been thinking of that since the moment I asked you to leave," he confessed.

When she caught his meaning, Ellen blushed violently and slapped his chest.

"You can keep thinking of that. You won't have a chance too soon," she told him in an upset tone of voice.

Still, Jay noticed the anxiety mixed with curiosity and desire in her eyes. *'Now, that's interesting,'* he mused. *'I think this woman has more surprises in store than I thought.'*

CHAPTER TWENTY

The following Saturday morning, Jay strode briskly into the low-rise building where Ellen lived. The man hadn't forgotten the longing in Ellen's eyes while she watched the lake from his balcony. That was why Jay had arranged with Becka and Bryan to go out on the lake that day. The couple had agreed immediately because Becka's parents wanted the babies for that entire Saturday.

Jay had told Ellen about his plans the previous night when he brought her home. First, he had taken Ellen out for dinner early in the evening. Then, they went to a musical and also wandered through the streets of the Entertainment District for a couple of hours afterward.

Ellen had been thrilled with Jay's invitation until the man warned her that he would come to pick her up at around seven in the morning. Jay still remembered the woman's grimace at his words, and he grinned.

Ellen wasn't a morning person. But then, Jay wasn't either. So, that was fine with him. As a matter of fact, he had found out that the two of them had a lot of things in common, although they butted heads regularly.

'What the heck, sparks just bring some more colour into my life,' he reflected.

Ellen and Jay had been going out together for an entire week already. They had spent whole days in each other's company, so Jay had learned a lot about the woman.

Every hour spent with Ellen had strengthened Jay's decision to keep her for himself. They were good together.

'Now, if only I had convinced Elle's strong head as well,' he mumbled with annoyance, climbing up the stairs to the fourth floor.

Although Jay wasn't particularly fond of waking up early in the morning, he insisted on having a private breakfast with Ellen, so he brought the food with him. He knew that Becka had planned a picnic at Bryan's lake house for later.

But then, Jay wanted to have Ellen just for himself for a couple of hours. He couldn't have enough of talking or playing with her. In the beginning, Ellen had been awkward at fooling around, but she learned.

The woman had grumbled when Jay presented his plan to her but accepted, and quite quickly. Besides being thrilled about going sailing, Ellen also seemed to enjoy being with Jay more and more without interference from the outside world.

Jay's hopes raised every minute. He couldn't wait until he made her his. The man might have had a moment of uncertainty concerning his success now and then, but he didn't allow doubt to flourish in his mind.

When he got to the fourth floor, Jay knocked briefly on Ellen's door and listened attentively. No sound of steps or anything else came from inside the apartment, and the man frowned for a moment. Then, he shrugged and knocked louder.

A moment later, something hit the front door, and he grinned. He could almost visualize how Ellen grabbed a shoe and threw it at the door.

Ellen hadn't woken up yet, but she had to. Jay decided that it was all right to knock again. He hit the door with his knuckles more insistently, and to his pleasure, Ellen's swearing reached his ears.

His brows shot up his forehead. The man hadn't thought that the woman would know those words. At least, she had never uttered them in his presence.

'So, you still have some secrets,' Jay grinned wolfishly and knocked again, with more determination.

"What?" Ellen shouted in an angry tone of voice from behind the door.

"Elle, sweetie. It's me, Jay," he said, barely keeping his laughter at bay.

"So?" she snapped, and he shook his head, smothering a chuckle.

"We were supposed to meet this morning," the man reminded her, making efforts to keep sober.

The woman swore again but unlocked the door. Although the blinds covered the windows, Jay had a full view of Ellen, and his gaze swept hungrily over her body.

The woman's honey-coloured hair stuck everywhere, and he stifled the impulse to brush his fingers through her dishevelled mane. A crease from the pillow was visible on her face. The woman's eyes were slightly puffy, and she rubbed them impatiently.

Ellen's so-called nighty covered her body only to the hips, and Jay's eyes zeroed in on her white cotton panties, which hugged her narrow hips snuggly. Besides, her nightgown was almost transparent, and the man didn't have any difficulty seeing what lay underneath. Then Jay delighted himself, sweeping his eyes over the expanse of her lithe limbs. He shook his head mentally.

Ellen didn't seem aware of his perusal. Half-asleep, she just waved him to get inside, and then she shuffled to the bathroom to take a shower.

The woman needed to feel human again. She had come back home at around two in the morning the other day, and usually, her body required more sleep than what she had.

Jay shook his head and grinned again. He closed the front door behind him and strode to the small kitchenette, which opened toward the studio.

Jay started to take the boxes with food out of the bag and lined them on the counter. When he got to the container with freshly ground coffee, he opened it and prepared the coffee.

Ellen's coffee maker was simple but efficient. *'Not like mine. I should have already replaced it. But then, I remember about that only when I make coffee,'* Jay shook his head ruefully.

The man had already finished setting the food on the coffee table. He gathered the bedsheets off the couch when Ellen's shout came from the bathroom.

"Jay, will you bring me the clothes I set on the armchair, please? I forgot about them."

"One moment, sweetie," he replied and then went back to folding the sheets.

He put them on one side of the sofa and then turned to the armchair. The night before, Elle had neatly laid a pair of jeans, a t-shirt, and a set of cotton underwear there.

Jay grinned and lifted the black panties with one finger. He looked at them from all sides and then picked up the bra, rubbing the cloth between his fingers.

"Jay," Ellen's impatient shout broke the spell.

'Get a hold of yourself, man,' Jay scolded himself. He grabbed the rest of the clothes and rushed to the bathroom.

"Here you are, sweetie," he knocked on the door.

Ellen cracked the door a little and slid her hand through the opening. She waved her fingers at him, and Jay gave her the clothes with a shake of his head.

The door shut in front of him with a bang, and he chuckled.

"I'll be out in a minute," Ellen said.

"Take your time," Jay replied, and then he went back to the studio and sprawled on the couch.

Ellen kept her promise and entered the room a minute later. Jay noticed that the woman hadn't taken the time to dry her hair thoroughly and shook his head in dismay.

"You should have dried your hair, Elle. I could have waited. It's not a problem."

"It doesn't matter. It will dry," Ellen waved her hand toward Jay. "I don't know how I didn't hear the alarm," the woman said and grabbed her cell phone off the coffee table to check it. "Apparently, I heard it," she grimaced. "And turned it off, of course," she snapped, upset with herself. "I'm sorry, Jay," she lifted her eyes at him, but the man merely shook his head with negligence.

"Don't worry about that, Elle," he waved his fingers. "Actually, I didn't mind at all. I love your nighty," he observed with a grin, and the woman slapped his shoulder. Jay laughed and pulled her next to him on the sofa. "Let's feed you before you turn into a ferocious kitten again."

Ellen turned her eyes to the coffee table. "Oh, gosh, did you think you would have to feed an army?" she exclaimed when her eyes laid on the food he had set out. *'How the heck I haven't noticed it so far?'* she wondered and then shifted her wide eyes at him.

Jay merely shrugged, and with a gesture, he invited her to start eating.

CHAPTER TWENTY-ONE

B ecka and Ellen leaned on the railing at the bow, talking and watching the lake. Now and then, their eyes would turn to Bryan and Jay, who were working together, handling Bryan's power yacht.

"I see how you're looking at Jay," Becka surprised Ellen with her words. "You do like him," Becka observed.

Ellen blushed and looked the other way. Becka laughed and shook her head in disbelief. "Did you really think that people wouldn't notice that you are in love with him?"

Ellen didn't say anything for a moment. She merely stared at a flock of birds that speared the horizon. Becka tilted her head, watching the other woman with curiosity.

"Do you think he is aware of that?" Ellen practically whispered her question.

Still, Becka heard her and shrugged. "He feels something, but I don't think he is sure that you love him. Men usually are a bit dense in that area. Besides, he is too close to you, and that makes it difficult for him to decipher what feelings you have for him."

"That's good," Ellen nodded with relief.

"Why?" Becka stared at Ellen with astonishment. "The man loves you. Why shouldn't he know what you feel for him? That you love him?"

Ellen's wide eyes turned to Becka, stunned because of her words. "What did you say?" she asked.

Becka shook her head again. "You don't know, do you?" she said softly. "You're also dense, Ellen. I am sorry to say that, but it's crystal clear. Jay is crazy about you, and he's never been this way," Becka gesticulated nervously. "Yes, we saw him with a woman now and then, but he always kept himself at a certain distance. He didn't want to get involved. With you...," she shrugged. "I don't know, but he seems like he wants to bind you to him and never let go. Maybe, I am not expressing this very well, but I hope you understand what I am trying to say," she pierced Ellen with a sharp gaze.

Unconvinced, Ellen nodded. She didn't dare to believe Becka. *Anyway, it's not like I would dream of happily ever after with Jay. I don't believe in such fairy-tales,'* she shrugged inwardly.

"How well did you get to know him?" Becka asked with curiosity.

"Quite well, I think," Ellen replied. "Well, as well as anybody can know somebody after spending practically every waking moment with that person for days in a row," she amended.

"Then, you do know him well. He must have shown his ugly side now and then," Becka laughed. "Anyway, no one's perfect," she shrugged. "You have a chance together," she continued earnestly. "Only if you can come to terms with his gambling problem, though."

"Jay doesn't have a gambling problem," Ellen pierced Becka with a dark gaze. "His reasons for playing cards are different."

"Oh, he told you then," Becka exclaimed loudly, drawing the men's attention.

"Shush, you don't know what you're talking about," full of anxiety, Ellen rushed to quiet Becka. *'Shoot! I couldn't keep my mouth shut, damn it!'* she scolded herself.

"What are you two talking about?" Jay asked and narrowed his eyes to slits, staring at Ellen.

"Nothing important," she waved his worries away and plastered a faint smile on her lips.

"Sorry, Elle, but you're lying," he replied in a challenging tone of voice. "Becka," he turned to his cousin, calling her name harshly.

"Jay, you won't take that tone with my wife," Bryan warned him with a dark look, and Ellen rubbed her palms off her jeans anxiously, watching Bryan with apprehension.

"Don't worry, Ellen," Bryan softened his voice noticing the woman's worry. "I won't ruin his pretty face," he chuckled.

"Hey, man, I'm not a girl," Jay shouted and hit Bryan in his arm with a fist.

"Jay," Ellen intervened immediately, striding toward the two men with angry steps. "Bryan's a fighter. You don't challenge a fighter, you idiot!"

"So, after you spilled the goods to Becka, you also attack my maleness," Jay observed, upset.

"I didn't spill anything," Ellen shook her head, but a blush betrayed her.

"Elle, Elle, Elle," Jay waved his finger to her to shut her down. "I told you that you don't know to lie convincingly."

The woman stomped her foot on the deck with irritation. She didn't know how the man guessed whenever she lied, but he did.

"All right, Jay," Becka came to them. "It's no big deal. You told her about your gifts. So? I also told Bryan," she pointed out, and Bryan nodded, putting his arm around her shoulders.

"I knew it," Jay turned to Ellen again. "You have a big mouth."

Ellen looked at him with disbelief, and then, she merely turned his back at him. "Becka, do you think that you have a plastic bag around?"

Becka's eyes rounded. "I hope you don't want to smother him even if he deserves it."

"I don't care about him," Ellen waved her hand with nonchalance.

"Oh, yeah, sweetie, you do," Jay intervened, and his voice sounded anxious.

Still, Ellen didn't pay any attention to him. She kept staring at Becka stubbornly and said in a flat tone of voice, "I was thinking of putting my things in a plastic bag and swimming back to the shore. I want to go home."

"Are you out of your mind, woman?" Jay burst furiously and grabbed her arm, turning Ellen to face him. "Who the hell is so crazy to cross the lake swimming?"

"Please, let go of my arm," she replied in a calm tone of voice.

He shook his head. "No, sweetheart. I can't let you do such a foolish thing. I'll handcuff you to me if I have to. And for what? Just because I said that you had a big mouth? You do, so get over it."

"Jay," Bryan warned him. "I'd shut up now if I were you."

"Why? I'm right. She's crazy. Why should I shut up?" Jay shouted, and Ellen's eyes narrowed dangerously.

"Because it's the smart thing to do," Bryan replied in a calm tone of voice. "If you don't want to lose her for good," he advised Jay, tilting his head toward Ellen, who was about to knee Jay in his weakest spot.

"All right, I shut up, but you stay put on the yacht," Jay turned his eyes back to Ellen, just in time to see her knee jerking up. "What the heck?" he yelled and jumped back, stumbling over a coil of ropes.

Jay fell down and pulled the woman with him. He had forgotten to free her arm. The man tried to cushion her fall, sliding his arms around her and rolling on his back.

"Are you all right, baby?" he started touching her everywhere with febrile movements, afraid that he had hurt her in his fall. Ellen didn't reply, and Jay panicked. "Sweetie, say something, please."

Bryan rolled his eyes and turned to his wife. "Have I ever been so pathetic?"

Becka smiled at him, and to the man's dismay, she nodded. "Once or twice. It seems to be a common affliction among men," she laughed.

"You'll pay for that, little imp," Bryan warned her with a meaningful look, and Becka's grin widened.

Then, the man turned to the couple still sprawling on the deck and sighed. Jay continued to talk a mile a minute, begging Ellen to speak to him.

"Jay," Bryan snapped. "Stop it, man. She's just got the wind knocked out of her. She needs a bit of air, not your constant lament," he scolded Jay and then returned to steering the yacht because they already were off course.

Jay gathered Ellen in his arms and helped her to sit up. Indeed, the woman panted, trying to draw air into her lungs.

"I'm sorry, sweetie," Jay stroked her jaw, turning her face to him in the process.

Ellen recovered after a couple of minutes and shook her head at him. "You're a wacky one, Jay."

"You're the wacky one, Ellen," Jay countered. "No one has ever thought of swimming across the lake," he shook his head.

"Yes, they have."

"Not this way," he replied.

"I know that. But sometimes, grave situations require out-of-the-box solutions," Ellen explained, leaning back on him.

"What was so grave, Elle?" Jay inquired with confusion. "I yelled at you, and you could have yelled at me. It was just a disagreement. If I had threatened your life, then yes, you'd have been right to think about jumping into the lake. But you know that I wouldn't ever touch you in anger, baby. I'm not made that way," he explained, stroking her arms.

"I know that. You like slashing people with your tongue," Ellen observed sarcastically.

"Yep, sometimes," Jay whispered in her hair.

"Most of the time," she retorted, shivering under his fingers.

"And that makes you run away from me?" the man asked, brushing his lips along the line of Ellen's neck.

"Not really," Ellen replied in a shaky voice.

"Then why swimming, my love?" Jay lifted a hand and turned her face up to him, staring at her, and an intense light glimmered in his black pupils.

"Honestly?" Ellen blushed. "Because I was feeling guilty. I don't have a big mouth, but what Becka said made me open my mouth without thinking," she confessed.

"And you decided to brave the lake," Jay shook his head in disbelief. "Sweetie, I roar, but only for a moment or two. What you did isn't such a big misstep. It happens. You should have just waited for me to see the light. It shouldn't have taken me more than a minute or two, even if I'm an idiot, as you always say," the man explained in a severe tone of voice.

"You're not an idiot," Ellen grimaced. "Just pigheaded," she pressed her lips.

Jay chuckled and leaned over her to kiss her lips. Bryan chose that very moment to say in a dry tone of voice, "We're at the island, people. Next time, Jay, maybe you choose to have your private conversation somewhere else where I can't see you." Ellen turned scarlet.

Jay shook his head and helped her to stand. "You have no tact, Bryan. You embarrassed Elle."

"Look who's talking," Becka burst into laughter.

"Anyway, let's get ready to get off the yacht," Bryan said, gazing at Jay meaningfully.

Jay led Ellen to the bench, where Becka had already taken a seat and joined Bryan. They started working on the sails, and in a few minutes, had the yacht deftly anchored in the marina.

Jay and Bryan gathered the bags and cooler to carry them to the shore.

They had just got to a bunch of trees not far from the shore and arranged the blankets for their picnic when Becka's cell phone rang. Bryan turned to her with inquiring eyes, and the woman shrugged, looking at the phone screen. "It's my mom. I don't know what she wants."

"And can't you answer and see?" Jay asked with a pointed look at the phone in her hand.

"Leave her alone," Bryan snapped. "Answer the call, Becka," he turned back to his wife.

"Hi, mom. Is everything all right?" Becka asked.

She listened to her mother's words, and her jaw dropped. "Oh, no. He'll have my head, mom," she cried out anxiously and then listened some more. "But I told you that in confidence," she shouted furiously. "It will be a hell of a day," she clenched her tiny fist, shaking her head impotently. "I don't care how I talk. I'm furious," she replied to her mother's scolding. "We'll talk later," she ended her discussion and turned off the phone.

"What's going on, Becka?" Bryan came to her, worried. He didn't like to see his wife so distressed.

Becka bit her lower lip and lifted her eyes to Jay, who watched her with apprehension. The man had the feeling that the call concerned him. He wasn't wrong.

CHAPTER TWENTY-TWO

"What the heck, Becka? Why did you have to tell her? You know that your mother gossips with everyone in the clan," Jay threw his hands in the air furiously.

"I don't know, Jay," Becka replied with tears in her eyes. "I just told her that you would come with your girlfriend to the lake. I didn't think she'd tell everyone."

Bryan hugged his wife from behind and shook his head to Jay, warning him to stop upsetting Becka.

"Maybe, it is better this way, Jay," he said quietly. "One day, you needed to introduce Ellen to everyone. It seems that today is that day. Just get used to the thought, man. Everyone goes through that, and it goes well in the end."

"But the witch will come," Jay practically roared.

"You must be more specific," Bryan grinned. "Which witch? Most of them are witches," he pointed out.

"Don't play with me, Bryan. You know who I'm talking about," Jay pointed his finger at the man.

"I know, but we can't do anything about it. Rebecca won't do anything to Ellen," Bryan tried to calm Jay down.

Ellen just looked from one at the other with apprehension. She understood that she should expect a clan gathering but didn't know how she felt about it.

"You know what she did to Nora," Jay barked.

Then, he noticed Ellen's wide eyes, and he closed the distance between them with giant steps. He took her in his arms and said, "Don't worry. I won't let her touch you. And this is a promise, baby."

"What did she do to Nora? And who is this witch?" Ellen's voice shook, and she drew back to look at the others.

In the ordinary course of events, nothing would have scared the woman. Nonetheless, they were talking about witches now, and all sorts of horrible things popped into her mind.

'How the heck can I protect myself from a witch?' she wondered.

"She just brought some rain, wind, and thunder over her head," Bryan waved her anxiety away. "She got wet, that's all. Jay exaggerates now because he worries about you."

"I can deal with some rain and thunder," Ellen lifted her eyes to Jay.

"You won't have to, baby. I won't let her touch you. Not even with a finger," he replied with determination.

"But maybe she'll want to shake hands with Ellen," Becka dried her tears and intervened in the conversation for the first time.

Jay threw a dark look in her direction and shook his head. "No, she won't touch Ellen," he repeated stubbornly.

Bryan shook his head and quieted his wife. Jay wasn't rational anymore, and Bryan started worrying. Irrational men provoked chaos in their wake.

"Let's start our picnic," Bryan proposed. "When did they leave?" he asked his wife.

"They left about an hour after we left," she replied in a small voice.

"Eh, we won't wait for them then. Let's eat, people."

"I'm not hungry anymore," Jay frowned.

"This is the first time you've ever said that," Ellen observed in bewilderment.

"I'm worried, woman," he snapped at her.

"You can eat if you want," she replied calmly. "Look, Jay, I know that I don't have all the information, and therefore, I shouldn't open my big mouth, as you like to say," she put up her hand to stop him when she saw that he wanted to say something. "But I know one thing," she continued in a flat tone of voice. "If you show your anxiety to someone, that person will take advantage of you. You need to be aloof and show that witch, whom I don't know, of course, that she can't touch you."

"That's the spirit, Ellen," Bryan chuckled. "She's right, you know," he turned to Jay. "Rebecca would grab the opportunity with both her hands if you show that you're afraid. Let's eat, Jay. When they get here, they'll find four people having fun, without a worry in the world," he thumped Jay on the shoulder and discreetly made a sign to Becka to start unpacking the food.

In the beginning, Jay just picked at his food, having lost any interest in their picnic. But then, Ellen drew him into their conversation, and the man started to be less tense and even enjoyed himself.

Bryan knew that Ellen would eventually find out about his first day on the island with Becka. So, he chose to relax the atmosphere by telling her what happened when he brought

Becka there for the first time. Ellen laughed so much that she had tears in her eyes, and Jay put his thumbs up to congratulate the man.

Jay still worried about what Rebecca would do once she laid her eyes on Ellen. He couldn't shake the feeling that something unpleasant would happen. Despite that, he joined the conversation, an arm around Ellen to keep her close to him.

"Anyways, this remains my favourite spot in the world," Becka remarked, leaning on Bryan, and the man grinned. He knew what she was talking about.

"You should take Ellen somewhere for a brief vacation," he advised Jay with a meaningful look. "I'm sure everything will turn out perfect."

"I thought about that," Jay nodded. "Ellen still has a couple of weeks to wait until she gets her private investigator license, so we could go on a brief vacation. What are you saying, sweetie?" Jay asked Ellen, looking down at her face.

Ellen nodded but didn't have the time to reply. Becka's eyes widened, and the woman tugged at Bryan's hand. Ellen's gaze turned to the lake because Becka was staring there. A yacht had just appeared in view and drew closer to the dock.

"The vultures appeared," Jay mumbled with annoyance.

Bryan looked at Jay nonplussed and then burst into laughter, shaking his head. "You're so dramatic, man," he observed.

Jay bad-mugged him and snapped, "Like you don't know what I'm talking about."

"Everything will be fine, Jay," Becka intervened. "You'll see."

JAY'S SALVATION

But Jay knew she was wrong. When Rebecca's voice reached his ears, he shook his head and grabbed Ellen's hand.

CHAPTER TWENTY-THREE

J ay refused to move off the blanket and welcome the newcomers. With a negligent shrug, the man had decreed that no one invited them there. So, he didn't have to extend any courtesy to any of them.

Bryan shook his head with disapproval and stood up with supple movements. He kept his eyes on the people striding toward them and noticed that Matt's jaw was set.

He concluded that Rebecca must have been in great shape that day. She was the only person in the whole world who would succeed in making Matt genuinely lose his temper.

"Your brother doesn't seem very happy," Bryan observed, turning to Jay.

"Of course, he isn't," Jay waved his hand with nonchalance. "He doesn't like the witch. I don't understand how she convinced him to bring her here," he wondered and pressed his lips in dismay.

"I understand that grandma threatened to hire a water taxi if Matt didn't want to take her on his yacht. Of course, Aunt Marjorie intervened and persuaded him to sail the old bat here on his boat," Becka replied.

"Poor Marjorie," Bryan shook his head. "She's always caught between those two stubborn people," he remarked ruefully.

Jay merely shrugged and started munching on a cookie nervously. Ellen touched his chest, and when he turned his eyes to her, she whispered, "Don't forget, Jay. Indifference is the best weapon."

Jay speared her with a black gaze but then nodded his agreement without much conviction.

'How the heck can I be indifferent?' he mused.

His grandma always made him feel inadequate. The woman looked at him as if he had been a blemish on the clan's reputation and disapproved of everything he did.

"You know, I don't get it," Jay suddenly said, and the others gazed curiously at him. "The old bat hasn't paid any attention to me for the last six or seven years," Jay continued with a wave of his hand. "Why the heck does she care about what I'm doing now?"

Becka shrugged. "Maybe she thinks that you hatched another scheme to get to the trust fund," she said negligently.

"Thank you, Becka," Jay snapped at her when he noticed Ellen's speculative gaze. "I haven't gotten around to telling Elle about that. I should have told her about everything else, of course, and you know I am not allowed."

"What are you talking about, Jay?" Ellen narrowed her eyes and looked at him with suspicion.

"Someone will tell her anyway," Bryan observed and shifted his eyes toward the group of people coming from the dock. They didn't hurry, and their strides matched Rebecca's gait.

"Remember that I told you not to listen to anything one of this bunch would say to you?" Jay said, tilting his head toward the group. "Well, this is the moment to show some confidence in me, sweetie. Just wait until I can tell you everything, all right?"

Ellen watched him pensively, and then she nodded. "I'll trust you for the moment, Jay. Don't make me regret it, though," she added in a stern tone of voice.

"You won't, I promise," he said quickly.

The group of people was close now. He could even see the thunder in Rebecca's eyes.

"Hello, mother," Jay said with a nod toward his mother, without abandoning his spot on the blanket. "Hey there, father. I didn't know you decided to crash our little picnic," he remarked in a mocking tone of voice.

"Watch your mouth, young man," Rebecca intervened harshly.

"Wow, grandma. It's been years since you haven't given me a sign that you were aware of my existence. What's with this change of heart you suddenly have?" the man replied in a challenging tone of voice, as well. But then, he didn't wait for her answer and turned to Matt. "Thanks, brother. Nice to know you always have my back," Jay said mockingly, although he knew that he was plain mean and unfair. Matt couldn't have refused their mother. Jay wouldn't have done it, either.

Matt pursed his mouth and clenched his fists, ready to give him a sharp reply. His wife touched his arm, though, and the man shifted his inquiring eyes at her. Nora shook her head, and Matt frowned.

"I see you haven't brought Nat with you, Nora," Jay noticed in a light conversational tone of voice.

However, he watched Rebecca from the corner of his eye at the same time. The old woman's expression darkened more and more, and she watched Ellen as if she were an insect.

'Yep, she'll explode any moment now,' Jay thought with satisfaction, although he wasn't sure that he had chosen the best course of action. He also didn't like the way his grandma was staring at Ellen.

"Nat is with his cousins," Marjorie spoke for the first time, spearing her younger son with a warning gaze. Jay used to be more polite, and she disapproved of his behaviour, although she understood why he reacted that way.

Jay knew that his mother referred to Becka and Bryan's twins, Leah and Sean. He guessed that they had left the boy behind so that he wouldn't witness the ugly scene Rebecca was bound to make. It sufficed that the kid had seen part of the awful discussion between his mother and Rebecca.

Ellen stole looks at everyone. Besides Jay's parents, Matt and Nora, and of course, Jay's grandma, there were two other young people in the group. She remembered that Jay had told her that he had a large family, and she surmised that the two must have been some of his cousins.

"I'm already tired," Rebecca said with a scowl for Jay. "If I remember correctly, there's a table with chairs on your patio, Bryan," she pointed her chin toward the man's house that could be seen through the trees.

"We're having a picnic here, grandma," Jay pointed out dryly. "We don't need a table."

"I do. Let's move there," the old woman ordered.

"But I feel well here," Jay retorted stubbornly, although he didn't know why he insisted on being rude to her. He didn't do anything else but invite more trouble.

"You'll feel good there too," Rebecca huffed. "Let's move," she barked.

Jay wanted to open his mouth again, but Ellen squeezed his hand and shook her head. "Let's go, Jay," she whispered and rose with fluid movements, tugging at the man's hand.

Sulking, Jay followed Ellen's example. They both helped Becka and Bryan gather the remnants of their picnic and the blankets.

The others started ahead, although Matt and Jonathan checked first if the four of them had everything in hand and didn't need their help.

Ellen waited until the other people started up the gentle slope of the hill toward Bryan's house, and then, she turned to Jay.

"That's not indifference, Jay. You're behaving like a brat," she scolded him. "You don't do anything else but show your grandma that you care about her opinion too much."

"I don't actually know what to do," the man confessed. "I just know that she'll say something to upset you, and you will leave," he confessed his greatest fear.

"Don't worry about that. I won't leave," Ellen reassured him.

"You want to leave whenever I say something," Jay reminded her.

"That's because it is you. I am not so sensitive to other people," the woman said, and a blush covered her face.

"Good to know," the man mumbled, and Bryan hid his smile.

He knew very well how it felt being in Jay's shoes. The man had gone through a similar thing, and that less than two years ago.

CHAPTER TWENTY-FOUR

Becka and Bryan laid the food and drinks on the table in a few minutes. Marjorie and Jonathan had brought some more food, and they helped the young couple set everything out.

When everyone found a seat and had a plate before them, Marjorie turned to Ellen.

"I'm afraid you don't know everybody, Ellen." Marjorie pointed to the older woman. "This is Jay's great-grandmother, Rebecca." Rebecca still looked at Ellen with displeasure.

Ellen nodded. She murmured a few polite words to Jay's grandma then. However, Rebecca didn't bother to answer but kept glaring at Ellen. The thunder in her pupils didn't promise anything good.

'Unpleasant woman,' Ellen reflected. *'She's looking at me as if I were an interloper,'* she shook her head slowly. Jay squeezed her hand and then pulled it in his lap. Ellen noticed the smile that appeared on the lips of the woman, sitting between Matt and Rebecca.

"This is Lily," Marjorie told Ellen. "Lily is Jay's cousin. Josh is her twin brother," Marjorie pointed to the young man that was sitting on the other side of Nora.

"I'm delighted to meet you, Ellen," Lily said with a warm smile. "It was high time Jay found someone to share his life," she continued and grinned at her cousin.

"Not so fast, young lady," Rebecca contradicted Lily. "We all know that Jay doesn't have any interest in sharing his life with Ellen. He merely wants my money," Rebecca turned her harsh gaze to Jay.

Enraged, Jay threw the fork he had in his hand on the table. The man jumped off his chair. He looked like he wanted to climb over the lawn table to strangle Rebecca.

Ellen tugged at his t-shirt. When he turned to her angrily, her brows arched, and she showed him to sit back in his chair.

The woman felt that Jay shook with rage. She took hold of his hand and intertwined her fingers with his. Jay breathed deeply, and Ellen felt the tension seep out of his body. "You're doing great, baby," she whispered.

Stunned, Jay turned his gaze to her. Although he used endearments for Ellen all the time, she had never uttered anything similar to him until then. Jay stared at Ellen, and his eyes sparkled with intensity. His gaze swept her face hungrily.

Ellen merely smiled at Jay, and her fingers flexed over his. Jay sat down, raised their joined hands to his mouth, and brushed his lips over the woman's delicate knuckles, always gazing insistently at her.

"You can't fool me with your theatrical show," Rebecca scoffed.

"Grandma," Marjorie warned her. "You should learn when you shouldn't talk," the woman said in a harsh tone of voice, and everyone looked at Marjorie with astonished eyes.

"You don't get to talk to me like that, girl," Rebecca snapped at Marjorie. "Do you think I'm stupid?" she turned to Jay afterward. "I won't hand you the money on a platter only because you put on a show before me," she said in a sarcastic voice.

"Grandma, you know where to shove your money," Jay replied in a dry tone of voice, and a few exclamations of bafflement filled the air.

Jonathan gasped, slapped his knee, and started laughing heartily while Marjorie shook her head in disapproval.

Matt put his thumbs up to congratulate his brother, and Josh laughed like a hyena. Bryan merely shook his head. He knew that the worst would come. He was right. Suddenly, black clouds gathered over their heads, lightning slashed the sky.

"Don't you think this trick is growing old, grandma?" Jay arched his brows sardonically. But then, he caught Ellen's hand and squeezed it to let her know that he wouldn't allow anything harmful to happen to her.

Rebecca's hard eyes pierced Jay with evident displeasure. She intended to give a harsh reply to the young man, but she didn't have the time.

"Yes, grandma," Matt intervened in a flat tone of voice. "We've already seen it. You didn't scare us with that stupid trick in the past, and you won't scare us now," he stared her down with his dark blue eyes.

The old woman frowned at Matt, and her lips turned into a pretty thin line. An ugly, malicious grin transformed Rebecca's features. She shifted her narrowed eyes toward Ellen and raised her hands with her fingers spread. The woman waved her fingers swiftly, and suddenly, Ellen's plate filled with a pile of grey mice, squirming one on top of the other. All around, mayhem ensued.

Ellen's eyes widened with horror. She paled and practically flew out of her chair, breathing hard and pressing a hand on her chest. She stifled a cry in her throat, pushing her fingers over her trembling lips.

Jay swore viciously and jumped up off his lawn chair as well with a sudden move. The chair fell to the ground with a loud bang. The man gathered the young woman to his chest, stroking her hair and back tenderly in an attempt to soothe her.

Nora hurried away from the table, her round eyes always on the squirming mice. Matt tried to catch her hand, but she shook her head. Nora waved at him to remain where he was so that he could take care of the problem. Matt disagreed with her, not very sure that he would succeed. However, with a demanding sign, Nora insisted. Matt resigned to remaining at the table in the middle of the chaos.

Everyone had started shouting at Rebecca at the same time. Becka practically attacked Rebecca, her eyes blazing. She didn't care about controlling her powers right then, and the wind swirled around them, blowing leaves into the air.

Becka's air flew in the wind, and Bryan had to restrain his wife, although he couldn't stop admiring her powerful beauty. However, the man was afraid that Becka would unleash her full powers and provoke a severe storm. His yacht was anchored at the dock, and Bryan would have loved to have it in one piece once that fight ended. So, he soothed his wife as best as he could.

When the wind tired down and disappeared, Bryan raised his reproachful eyes to Rebecca, shaking his head in disbelief. He looked at the old woman as if he saw her for the first time, and the woman merely scoffed at him.

The woman focused her narrowed eyes on the couple and didn't pay any attention to anyone else. Rebecca didn't look like she had cared about the scandal she had stirred. She discounted Bryan as not crucial for the moment and shifted her gaze from him to Ellen and Jay.

However, while Becka got lost in her own storm, Lily and Josh had lashed out with resentment toward the old lady. The twins were sick and tired of the old woman's schemes. They couldn't understand how their great-grandma's mind worked anymore. But then, their words fell on deaf ears.

By then, Jonathan had joined the fray as well. Rebecca treated him with the same indifference she would have shown to an annoying fly. She only fluttered her hand to the man to make him shut up. The woman knew that Jonathan didn't represent a valuable contender in that discussion because he didn't have any powers to fight against her.

Only Marjorie hadn't joined the scandal. She had shaken her head with sadness, watching the uproar for a few minutes, and then, she rushed to Ellen's side, intending to check on her.

Immediately, Jay turned to his mother furiously and shouted at her. "You had to bring her here. When the hell will you learn? She's a spiteful dried-up woman, and she can't live if she doesn't spread her unhappiness around," the man ground his teeth.

Marjorie attempted to say something, but Jay didn't give her a chance. He stretched his arm and stopped her from getting closer to Ellen. Then, his eyes speared his mother with a stony gaze, and he added in a quiet but resolute tone of voice, "You've done enough for now. I'll take Elle and move out of the province to get rid of the lot of you."

Ellen gasped in shock. The young woman had just recovered from her fright and caught Jay's last words. She tugged at his shirt and whispered, "No, Jay, you won't."

Jay quieted her, stroking her face. "I said that no one would get to touch you, Elle. That was a promise, which I didn't keep, baby. But I will keep it from now on. If we have to leave this city, we'll do it."

"No one touched me, Jay," she shook her head, gazing insistently into the man's eyes. "You kept your promise."

Jay engulfed Ellen in his arms and buried his face into her hair, grateful for her understanding.

Marjorie watched them with sadness. Jay's words had brought tears in her eyes, and now, they ran freely on her face.

Jay's words reached Jonathan's ears, and the man strode in a hurry to his wife at once. The man slid his arm around her quivering shoulders and brought her to his chest.

"Don't worry, Jay won't leave," he told his wife in an undertone, wiping her tears off with his thumb.

Matt had narrowed his eyes to slits and observed everything. Rebecca's actions had enraged him already, but when his mother began crying, his rage reached the boiling point. He threw his hands in the air and shouted, "Hey, all of you. Shut up, that's enough."

His harsh tone of voice put an end to the uproar. Matt's outbursts were so rare that people listened when he roared.

Everyone turned to Matt, watching him inquiringly. Matt took a deep breath and then said, "That's what we're going to do."

CHAPTER TWENTY-FIVE

"You, all, get back to your chairs and stop quarrelling," Matt said, and his tone of voice didn't invite to replies. Jay opened his mouth to retort, and Matt shook his head with determination.

"That's valid for you too, Jay. Take Ellen and get a seat far from that plate with... You know what I mean," the man showed Jay to move their chairs to the other end of the table. "Lily, take care of those mice. You're the best at those stupid spells. I'm sick of watching them," he grimaced, waving his fingers toward Ellen's plate. "Make the plate disappear too. I don't think that Bryan would want it anymore," he said, glancing inquiringly at Bryan.

The man nodded with conviction in complete agreement with Matt. Only the thought of using that plate in the future made him feel sick in the stomach.

Matt pressed his lips, watching around with searching eyes. Then, he turned to his wife. "Nora, will you bring other plates for Ellen and Jay? I'd ask Becka, but she's still vibrating with anger, and I'm afraid that she'd break the damned things."

"Of course, Matt," his wife smiled at him. She passed by him on her way into Bryan's house and whispered, "I knew you could bring order to chaos, love."

The woman reached up and touched her mouth to Matt's briefly. Afterwards, she went to the house to bring the dishes.

Matt looked after his wife until she entered the house. Then, he breathed deeply once more and turned to Rebecca. She was watching everything with a frown on her face.

"I'm calling a water taxi for you," he said to his great-grandmother in a demanding tone of voice. "It's time that you went home," Matt glared at the old woman. "From now on, try not to come to any outings if you hear that I'm present," the man warned her. "And stay away from my family and especially from my brother."

"You won't call me any taxi," Rebecca speared him with thunder in her eyes. "I'm not ready to leave."

"Yes, you are," Matt countered in a tone that didn't invite any more discussions. Then he took his cell phone out of his pocket and called the owner of a water taxi service, one of his clients.

"Hey, man," Matt said when his call was answered.

His cold gaze never left Rebecca's face. Stunned, the woman was watching him. She couldn't believe that he was going through with his threat.

"Matthew Winston here. I need a water taxi to my cousin's island to pick up my grandma," he continued and then gave the coordinates to the man. "I'll pay for both ways, no worries," Matt assured him. "Thanks."

He disconnected the call and said to no one in particular, "That's settled."

"You don't get to order me around," his grandma huffed.

"You'll leave. As soon the taxi gets here," Matt replied with quiet intensity. "Even if I have to hogtie you, you will leave."

"Marjorie," Rebecca turned to her granddaughter. "Talk to him," she ordered with a bark.

However, Marjorie shook her head at the woman's request. "No, I won't. You've done enough bad things today," she said, and Jonathan supported her decision.

Marjorie's reply shocked the old woman. She hadn't expected that answer from her granddaughter.

"Marjorie," she said in a warning tone of voice. "Your father will hear about your impertinence."

"I'm sure grandpa will get over it," Jay intervened harshly, fed up with his great-grandma's presence. "Sweetie, let's walk on the shore that way," he pointed to a trail leading away from the dock. "We'll return once the witch left," he whispered to Ellen, and she shook her head with a smile. "Don't you want to go away from here for a few minutes?" Jay asked her with astonishment.

"I don't want Rebecca to think that she has any power over you," Ellen whispered back to him. "We'll remain here to see her leaving," she decided.

Jay merely shrugged and slid his arm around her shoulders. He admired the woman. Ellen had a strong backbone.

"It still remains that issue with the money," Rebecca intervened in a dry tone of voice, and everyone groaned.

Jay retorted, staring the old woman down, "As I've already said, I make my own money. On Monday morning, talk to your lawyers to take my name out of your trust." Then the man added in a stern tone of voice, "And you can erase me from your memory, as well. I've had enough of you. I won't be present in the same room with you from now on. I don't want to ever lay my eyes on you. Is it clear?"

"You say so now," Rebecca scoffed, waving her hand. "But I know better. You won't give up your part of the trust. I know what you're able to do to get your greedy hands on my money. I haven't forgotten Camilla," she replied triumphantly, watching Ellen with mean eyes.

"Camilla?" Ellen whispered to Jay. "I think I want to hear about that."

"Not a problem, young lady," Rebecca intervened, proving that her hearing was as strong as ever. "I can tell you all about her."

"No, thanks," Ellen replied in a quiet tone of voice. "Jay will do it just fine, and not now."

Rebecca narrowed her eyes, and Matt barked, "Until the taxi gets here, take a seat, grandma, and stop badgering Ellen."

"I don't speak to you anymore," the old woman turned to him furiously.

"But you won't speak to me either," Jay didn't forget to mention.

"I have no intention to talk to you. I want to tell Ellen about Camilla," she said.

"I don't think so," Ellen shook her head. "If Jay has anything to tell me about that subject, he'll do it. Besides, after the mice thing, I don't feel like talking to you either," the young woman pointed out in a hard of voice.

"Good for you," Bryan approved of her decision.

"So you rallied against me as well," Rebecca turned to him with narrowed eyes.

"This time, you've done it," Bryan replied quietly.

"And you're escalating," Lily pointed out. "I quite expect that you'd turn the man I date in a frog if you get a whiff of that."

"You know that I want the best for you," Rebecca replied.

"The problem is that you don't know what the best is," Jonathan intervened swiftly. "You think you do, I'll give you that, but you're wrong every single time. You were wrong about Amelie and me. You were also wrong about Bryan and Nora," he pointed out. "You admit that you were wrong only when it is too late," he shook his head with regret.

"You don't know what you're talking about," Rebecca snapped at him.

"But I do know. I know my boys, Rebecca," he said, gazing between Matt and Jay. "They won't forgive you. Congrats, grandma. You managed to split the family," Jonathan said with sadness.

"I haven't done anything of the kind," she retorted. "Marjorie, tell your husband to watch his mouth."

"No, she shouldn't," Nora intervened in conversation. "Jonathan is correct. Matt will not talk to you anymore. I worked hard to make him accept your presence, grandma. You ruined it. And from what I see on Jay's face right now, he won't forgive you soon if ever."

"Better said never," Jay speared the air with a firm gesture.

Rebecca frowned and turned to Ellen with a pointed look.

"Don't look at me," Ellen shrugged. "I respect Jay too much, so I won't try to change his mind. Besides, I'm not the forgiving type of woman. Sorry," she said, but her tone of voice showed that she was far from being sorry.

Rebecca pursed her mouth and narrowed her eyes more. She noticed the satisfied smile on Jay's lips and thundered him with his eyes. The man merely shrugged and decreed, "Now, I'm hungry. Let's eat, people."

Everyone burst into laughter, except Rebecca, and Ellen pulled the man's head toward her and kissed him full on the mouth.

"You're fantastic, Jay," she whispered to him when she drew back.

"Good to know you think of me like that," he replied mischievously.

"Give me some of Bryan's chicken," Josh waved his hand toward Jonathan, who was closer to the side of the table where the chicken lay.

"Leave some for me, man," Jay frowned at his cousin.

"Not so fast," Rebecca intervened.

"That's your favourite expression from what I can see," Josh looked at his great-grandma with indifference. "Anyways, I'm hungry, so make it fast, Uncle Jonathan."

CHAPTER TWENTY-SIX

E veryone breathed with relief once Matt escorted Rebecca
to the water taxi, and they saw the back of the old woman.
She had spewed all sorts of threats, but no one really cared
about what she had to say anymore. Not even the patient
Marjorie or the understanding Nora didn't think to side with
Rebecca.

With her departure, the tension within the group
vanished. The people returned to picking at their food and
talking all at the same time.

However, Bryan felt his heart cringe when he thought that
beneath her anger, sadness must have laid, as well. He got closer
to knowing her during the last few months, and Rebecca was
not really a wicked person. Still, she had a particular opinion
about how people should have lived their lives. Until she was
proven wrong, which apparently happened all the time,
Rebecca stuck to her convictions.

Becka looked at Bryan and clasped his hand. Bryan turned
his gaze to her and shook his head, letting her understand
that nothing was the matter. Then, he brushed his lips off her
knuckles tenderly and said,

"Becka, you were amazing out there, baby. I must confess that, for a few moments, you took my breath away. However, I'd have liked it more if you had shown a little care about the yacht," he approached the thumb to the index to illustrate his words.

Josh heard his words and laughed. "Yeah, Becka was on the wave. Good for you, Becka," he tilted his head to see his cousin better. "I was afraid that you had become too tame," the man waved his hand. "You know, getting married, and becoming a mom, and all that."

"I'll show you how tame I am," Becka speared him with her narrowed eyes.

"Didn't you have enough of disputes today?" Matt inquired in a dry tone of voice, and Jonathan chuckled.

"Anyway," Lily intervened. "I hope you don't worry too much about what grandma said," she spoke to Ellen.

"She won't do anything else to you, so you shouldn't worry," the redhead shook her head, and her shiny coppery hair bounced.

"That's true," Marjorie nodded. "Rebecca was against Nora initially, and now she loves her," the woman pointed out. "And the same thing happened to Bryan," she turned her eyes toward the blond giant. "Now, I've heard her several times saying *I will have to ask Bryan,*' whenever she needed to make a difficult decision."

"As if I cared who she loves or not," Jay scoffed. "Grandma won't get another chance to touch Elle," he replied in a resolute tone of voice. "I was very serious when I said that we would move out of the province," he pointed out.

"You might have been serious, Jay," Ellen intervened. "But then, you forgot to ask me what I wanted," she pointed out, and all eyes turned to her.

"I'm asking you now," Jay made a point of saying, gazing at her with sharp eyes. "What do you want, Elle?"

Jay practically held his breath. He feared that the woman's answer would make all his hopes crash.

"First of all, I should tell you what I don't want," Ellen stressed out, levelling her eyes squarely on him. "I won't agree that you break your ties with your family. Your family is close-knit, Jay. I'll never accept that you moved away from your parents, brother, and cousins, even if your line of work allows you to live anywhere. Besides, you love this city," she waved her hand in the direction of Toronto, which lay beyond the water.

"I'll learn to love another town too. I think that Montreal or Vancouver would suit me," Jay observed, and Marjorie gasped in dismay.

Vancouver was too far away, and she wouldn't have seen her son too often. Her hand shook, and her cutlery clanked on the plate.

Jonathan stroked her arm to quiet her fears, and Ellen shook her head.

"You're distressing your mother, Jay. No, I won't move either to Montreal or Vancouver," Ellen said with determination. "I like it here in Toronto. And another thing, Jay. I don't understand why you would give satisfaction to Rebecca. By showing her that she can make you run out of the town with your tail between your legs," she looked at him inquiringly.

"I'm not running away," Jay replied in a huff, although, inwardly, he admitted that he was doing just that.

"Then, you'll remain in Toronto," Ellen beamed at him. "That's good to know."

"What would be the point to leave without you?" the man shrugged.

"That's what I was thinking," Matt chuckled. "Ellen's right," he told his brother. "You shouldn't give Rebecca the satisfaction to chase you out of the town," the man shook his head.

"And don't worry, Jay," Jonathan intervened. "Once she sees how good you are together, Rebecca will stop doing anything."

"She won't see anything," Jay leaned forward and stressed his words. "I was very serious when I said that I don't want to see her anymore," the man pointed out. "Anyway, we should go on vacation, Elle. You still have to wait for that license and have time to kill," he argued.

Ellen shook her head. "I'm sorry, Jay, but I can't go anywhere. My savings are stretched as it is, and I don't know when I'll find work again," she replied morosely. She wouldn't have accepted to live on someone else's money.

"Why don't you establish your own company?" Matt asked her, watching her with speculation in his eyes. "I often work with individuals that work for themselves and set up a company just because it is easier with the taxes afterward."

"I've thought about that," Ellen admitted. "But then, who hires a newbie?" she raised her hands.

"You're not a newbie," Matt pointed out. "You've been a police officer for some years and raised to the status of detective. I would hire you without questions," he shrugged.

"And I can also recommend you to other people. My colleagues need investigators all the time. Besides, someone from one of the major insurance companies just told me they needed to hire another private investigator. The guy they worked with had moved out of the province. And please, note, this offer stands, regardless of your future relationship with Jay," Matt took care to mention.

"What the heck, Matt?" Jay frowned and jumped off his chair.

'Sit down," Matt ordered to him in a quiet tone of voice. "Ellen needs to know that she has choices, and she does," the man turned his sharp eyes to the woman. "I don't want you to feel that if you choose to accept my help, it means that you have to remain with Jay or that Jay might think that you stayed with him because of that. My offer is independent of your relationship. If you choose to walk out of him right now, my offer still stands. If you marry him tomorrow, the same. Is it clear?" he asked her, and Ellen nodded.

No one said anything for a couple of minutes. Ellen started feeling conspicuous when the silence stretched for a longer time.

Jay, always attuned to her emotional state, broke the silence. "That means that your savings are not in jeopardy, Elle," he said in a dry tone of voice. "So, you can very well agree to go on vacation with me for a few weeks. Anyway, I would have taken care of the hotel and meals," he warned her. "You know that I'm old-fashioned in that matter," he shrugged.

Ellen looked at him from under her lashes and bit her lower lip. Jay chuckled and shook his head.

"No worries, you'll have your own room," he said, and Ellen blushed. He approached his head closer to her and whispered, "I know better than to rush into some things, baby. You shouldn't worry."

His words reached Jonathan, though, and the man laughed.

"Shut up, Jay," Embarrassed, Ellen snapped and slapped the man's thigh.

Jay merely shrugged. "Anyways, I was thinking of the Georgian Bay," Jay mentioned. "It looks awesome at this time of the year, from what I read, even though people prefer it in summer."

"Oh, yes," Marjorie said pensively. "It looks great in autumn. Do you remember?" she turned to Jonathan, her eyes sparkling with a new light.

The man chuckled softly and brought Marjorie's hand to his lips. "How could I forget it?" he whispered.

Ellen watched them nonplussed, feeling awkward to witness their feelings. She looked around and noticed that she was the only one. The others didn't see anything out of the ordinary.

Nora observed Ellen with an amused smile in the corners of her mouth. She knew how the woman felt because she'd been there just a little while ago.

"All right, Jay," Ellen decided that it was time to break the moment when her eyes fell on Nora's amused smile. "I'll go with you to the Georgian Bay. I haven't been there before, after all," she shrugged.

JAY'S SALVATION

As a matter of fact, Ellen had seldom been anywhere. Her childhood and adolescence didn't abound in happy days, and her adulthood hadn't offered too many chances to go out.

"But first, tell me about Camilla," she said in a dry tone of voice.

CHAPTER TWENTY-SEVEN

T he woman had the feeling that she wouldn't like what the man had to say. He stared at her nonplussed.

Josh burst into laughter, and Lily elbowed him to make him stop. Everyone else around the table just stared at Ellen with almost the same expression on their faces.

"Camilla's just one blip on my tormented youth," Jay finally said with a shrug.

"She must have been a serious blip, though," Ellen couldn't stop to remark. "Otherwise, Rebecca wouldn't have mentioned her."

Jay grimaced. The man didn't know what to do. On the one hand, Jay had to keep the secret regarding the conditions to get the trust money. On the other, he was afraid of what Ellen would say, hearing about his shortcomings.

Jonathan sensed that Jay felt between the devil and the blue sea. The man turned toward Marjorie and arched his eyebrows.

The woman nodded and said, "Jay, I understand you're not interested in the trust money anymore."

"Yes, mom, that's true," Jay agreed. "You know very well that I don't need her money. All the awards I won during the last four years and the royalties I regularly get for my series offer me a way to comfortable living," he shrugged. "I don't need grandma's money anymore," he shook his head.

"Then, you should explain everything to Ellen," Marjorie waved her hand.

"Allow me to do it," Josh grinned wolfishly. "I'm sure I can explain everything with much more accuracy than you."

"Shut your mouth, Josh," Jay snapped.

"Maybe you should tell her about the conditions of the trust first," Bryan noted in a quiet tone of voice."

"I intend to," Jay mumbled. "But I don't know how to start," he admitted.

"If you want, I can explain that part," Marjorie offered, watching Jay expectantly.

"Be my guest," the man waved his hand. "I'm sure you can explain that part better than I."

"Well," Marjorie joined her hands on the top of the table after she pushed her plate aside. "Ellen, I don't know if you know, but my grandmother had decided to curse the young generations as a result of some disappointments she had the misfortune to have."

"She knows about the curse, mother," Jay fluttered his hand impatiently.

"Oh, good then. I will explain to you the part with the trust," Marjorie smiled at Ellen. "Grandma put all her money in a trust, you see. The condition to get the money is to prove that you love someone and are fully committed to the person you love. However, that person must love you and is committed to you, as well," Marjorie explained.

"How can she determine that?" Ellen's eyes rounded.

"She doesn't," Bryan intervened in a dry tone of voice. "But then, she appointed two trustees that are mind readers. They determine if a couple tells the truth or not. I've been there and know how it is," he grimaced.

"Oh, I see now," Ellen nodded.

"You accepted everything easier than I did," Nora observed, and Ellen blushed.

"I showed her some of the things I could do before today," Jay confessed, and Matt smiled.

"You were smarter than I," he remarked. "I had a hell of a time with Nora when she found out about our talents," he recollected, turning his eyes to his wife.

"It wasn't so easy to swallow," she said dryly.

"Oh, Elle didn't fuss or anything," Jay waved his hand, proud of her.

"Aha," the woman mumbled. "Now, about that Camilla," Ellen arched an eyebrow, and Josh chuckled.

"You're not off the hook yet, Jay," he noticed.

"You're a real pain in the... back," he edited his words when he saw his mother's expression. "Anyway, I'll tell you, Elle," Jay took hold of the woman's hand.

'I won't probably like what he has to say,' the woman mused. *'That's why he turned on the charm.'*

"Yep, sweetheart, it is not too pretty, I admit," Jay said, feeling her emotions.

'I sense what she feels with astonishing accuracy,' he marvelled. *'I wonder what else I'm capable of doing now that I love her.'* However, the man shrugged inwardly and continued with his explanation.

"When I was about twenty-two, I decided that I needed the trust money. I wanted to buy everything necessary to create great comics."

"In the end, you did it, son," Jonathan noticed. "And without the help of Rebecca's money," he pointed out.

"You should know he has already won several awards," Marjorie said proudly. "Joe Shuster Award, Doug Wright Award... This year, he won the Eisner Award."

"Thank you, mom, but Elle doesn't need a list with all my awards," Jay noticed dryly. "Anyway, at the time, I thought to try my luck with the trust money," he shrugged. "I convinced a girl, Camilla, to pose as my lover, and we went to grandma," Jay shook his head in dismay.

"And a lot of good did that to you," Lily intervened. "Of course, the mind-readers busted you right away," she laughed softly. "And that girl," she shook her head. "Camilla was probably the worst actress in the whole world," Lily gestured broadly.

"And stupid to the boot," Josh didn't fail to remark. "We had a lot of fun at Jay's expense then and afterward," he pointed out.

Jay shrugged with indifference. Still, he worried about what Ellen would say, and his heart cringed, waiting for her reaction.

"Now, I understand why Rebecca treated me that way," Ellen said pensively.

"Ah, no," Bryan replied. "She did the same thing to Nora and to me."

"To everyone," Jonathan intervened. "She did it to my sisters-in-law and to me too. So, Jay's venture didn't make her the way she is," he said.

"Anyway, I'm wiser now, and I know that I don't need her money to succeed," Jay mentioned.

"From what I hear, you have already succeeded," Ellen replied, squeezing his hand. "And I think that you needed just talent."

CHAPTER TWENTY-EIGHT

Ellen and Jay returned at the end of the first week of November. That was only because Matt had announced to Ellen that all her documents were in order now, and she could start working any time.

Jay had kept postponing their return date before. Now, he regretted that their interlude at the Georgian Bay ended.

However, Ellen noted that the end of their vacation didn't mean that they wouldn't spend time together anymore.

"You can count on that, baby," Jay assured her in a determined tone of voice.

In fact, the connection between the two of them had become stronger during their vacation. Jay taught the woman how to have fun, and Ellen taught him how to slow down and enjoy a quiet evening in two.

Jay's powers had suddenly developed, and the man stopped feeling the need to prove anything to himself. As a result, he didn't think of gambling even once. He preferred strolling with Ellen or taking her out for a dance.

Ellen started working on various small assignments, but she spent every spare moment of the day or evenings at Jay's.

Jay caught up with his work while she was out in one of her investigations. He had a deadline coming soon and still had to work on his latest book in the series.

On November 21st, Ellen and Jay went to court for the first day of the trial against the casino owner. Matt had told them that he would be waiting for them in front of the building behind Osgoode Hall. He had another criminal case before Jay's.

Ellen and Jay crossed the street to the Court House, and Matt waved at them. The moment the couple stepped on the pavement, a gunshot resounded in the street.

Under Matt's shocked eyes, Ellen fell to the ground, bringing Jay down with her. The man had his arm over her shoulder tightly, and inertia pulled him down as well.

Around them, people started shouting and running for safety. Matt watched everything with horror in his eyes. His pupils had invaded the dark blue of his irises.

Two police officers only got out of their car when the woman was shot in front of the building. They saw the shooter, a tall, thin man with a hood over his head, and ran to apprehend him.

Their move stirred Matt from his shock, and the man rushed to Ellen and Jay. He knelt next to them, scared out of his mind.

Ellen lay on the pavement with her eyes closed. Her eyelashes touched her pale skin, and her lips had lost their colour.

Jay was frantic. The man had pressed his hand on the woman's wound, although he wasn't sure of what he was doing. Matt took his phone out of his pocket and called for an ambulance, putting a hand on Jay's shoulder for support.

JAY PACED THE WAITING room nervously. He glanced at his watch the fourth time in half an hour and gnashed his teeth.

Matt had called Nora and his parents, and now, they huddled in the corner of the room, whispering and gazing at Jay with worry. The young man looked more dishevelled than usual, and he kept pacing the room, clenching his fists.

No one dared to approach him. The hard thin line of his mouth didn't invite anyone to talk.

"Are you sure the EMT said that she'd be fine?" Marjorie asked her older son again. She feared for Jay's state of mind if anything terrible had happened to Ellen.

"I'm sure, mother," Matt repeated, rolling his eyes. The woman had asked that question a few times already. However, he worried as well. He didn't have to imagine what his brother felt because he had been in his situation.

Two police officers entered the room and eyed everyone attentively. When their gazes laid on Jay, they exchanged a glance. They decided to go to Matt instead and avoid the young man.

"Officer Stark and Petrovski, sir," one of the men said quietly, waving his hand to indicate who was who. "We wanted to let you know that the shooter is under arrest. He already confessed to everything and indicated who put the contract on the lady's head."

"That's good," Matt nodded. "Then, you have the other man in custody, as well, I presume," he said in a harsh tone of voice.

One of the officers, Petrovski, grimaced, and the other one shook his head. When Matt narrowed his eyes, Officer Stark rushed to say, "A few officers are on their way to arrest him right now, sir. The man will be arrested soon, don't worry. We couldn't be part of that team as we two witnessed the shooting. We will have to testify in court," he took care to point out.

"Right," Matt approved. "Then, I'll see you in court. I want an ironclad case," he warned them.

"It will be, no worries," Petrovski replied, and with a brief wave of the hand, turned to the door and left.

"Do you have him? The shooter," Jay stepped in front of him, cutting his way out.

"Yes, sir, he's arrested," Petrovski replied in a confident tone of voice.

"You'll take care of him," Jay said in a stern tone of voice.

"We've already taken care of him, sir," Stark intervened.

"Good then," Jay nodded and stepped aside to let them pass.

Then, he noticed the doctor coming into the room and forgot everything about the officers. The man hurried to speak to the surgeon.

"How is she?" Jay asked and clenched his fists again. His fingers shook, and he didn't want that the others noticed his state.

"She's fine," the doctor waved his hand. "The surgery went well, and we removed the bullet. It stopped into the shoulder blade and didn't do much damage. As you requested, your girlfriend will be transferred to a private room, and you can visit her there in about ten minutes. A nurse will show you the way," the doctor said.

"Thank you," Jay managed to murmur. "How long will she be in the hospital?" he inquired.

"Depending on her evolution today and tomorrow, she might be out of here by Thursday or Friday," the man answered.

Jay nodded to show that he understood and shook the surgeon's hand. The moment the doctor left, the others gathered around Jay.

"She will be fine, son," Jonathan thumped him over the shoulder. "She'll be home with you before your birthday," he smiled.

Jay nodded and murmured, "Thank God for that."

CHAPTER TWENTY-NINE

J ay chose to spend his birthday only with Ellen. She had just come out of the hospital the day before. Jay had asked her to take the second bedroom of his apartment.

Ellen needed help, and Jay didn't feel comfortable knowing her alone in her studio. It took some convincing, but the man had persuaded her in the end.

During the last two months, Ellen had found out many things about Jay. However, she hadn't learned about his birthday until the morning of November 26th, when his phone started ringing like crazy.

While they were having breakfast early in the morning, Jay's parents called to wish him *Happy Birthday*, and calls from his brother, uncles, and cousins followed.

'I should have guessed,' Ellen reflected in dismay. *'His cell phone pin number is 2611. I should have thought that it was his birthday,'* she frowned, and her mouth turned into a thin line.

"Are you all right, sweetie?" Jay asked her with concern, squeezing her hand.

Ellen nodded and smiled faintly at him. "I didn't know it was your birthday," she replied morosely.

Jay chuckled softly and teased her, "You didn't check so far?"

Ellen tilted her head. "Don't be mean," she slapped his arm playfully. "No, I haven't checked so far. I wasn't interested in your age at that time," she confessed. "How old are you today?"

"Twenty-nine," Jay said with a smile. "Just one year shy of the big thirty," he bobbed his eyebrows at her, and she laughed.

"Happy birthday, baby," Ellen whispered then, and she leaned toward him. She kissed his lips softly and wanted to pull back, but Jay's intentions were different.

The man slid his arm around Ellen to keep her close to him, and his intense gaze searched the woman's eyes. Then, he brushed his lips over the side of her face and her neck. Jay lifted his eyes at her again, and with a wolfish smile, he kissed her mouth hard.

The man pulled back and noticed, "You know, Elle, this is just the second time you've called me that."

The woman watched him with wide eyes for a few seconds, and then she shrugged. "It doesn't come easily to me," Ellen admitted. "That doesn't mean that...," she started to say but stopped.

"Don't leave me like this," Jay groused, frustrated. "That doesn't mean," he waved his hand to show to Ellen that she should continue.

The woman blushed and shrugged again. "I wanted to say that I'm fond of you," she replied in a small tone of voice.

"Just fond of me?" Jay leaned over her anxiously. He arched his eyebrows, waiting for her to say something.

"Do I have to say it?" Ellen snapped at him.

"It's my birthday, after all," he grinned mischievously.

"That it is," she nodded. "And I didn't know about it, so I don't have a gift for you," she replied morosely.

"But you have, Elle," Jay insisted and then tugged at her hand. "We've finished here, haven't we?" he perused the breakfast table to check if Ellen had already eaten everything. "Let's go into the living room," he proposed.

"But we have to clean the table," Ellen protested.

"We don't have to do anything, sweetie," Jay shook his head. "We can do it later. Let's go to the sofa and talk about your gift to me," Jay said gruffly, standing up, and Ellen blushed again.

When the man tugged at her hand again, Ellen stood up and followed him into the living room. Jay helped her sit on the couch, and then he sat next to her. He slid his arm around the woman and gathered her to him.

"Now, I need the words," Jay whispered in her hair.

"Can't you just read my emotions?" she huffed.

"That I could," Jay nodded. "But then, I'd still want to hear your words, so there's no point in prying through your emotions," he shrugged. "Come on, Elle, don't be mean. It's my birthday," the man said again.

Ellen shook her head but smiled. *He's just like a little boy right now,* she reflected.

"All right, Jay, here it goes," she said and bit her lower lip. "And that only because it is your birthday. I'm not used to saying something like that regularly," Ellen warned him.

"And I appreciate that, sweetheart. I'd prefer that you didn't say that to anyone else," he pointed out.

"You're so funny," the woman mumbled with annoyance.

"No, I'm honest. I don't want you ever say anything like that to another man," Jay stressed out, his dark eyes gazing at her with a quiet intensity.

A shiver crossed Ellen's body, and her hand flew to her throat. "I have no intention to say these words to any other man, Jay," she replied softly. "Who would be interested in another man when you are around?" she wondered, shaking her head. Then, she raised her hand to Jay's jaw, looked into his eyes, and whispered, "I love you, baby."

Jay had been holding his breath impatiently, and now, he exhaled loudly and said, "Thank God." Then, he leaned over Ellen and practically kissed her savagely, crushing her to his chest.

A cry flew off her lips before his mouth settled over hers. However, Jay was so lost in passion that he didn't notice. Ellen squirmed a little in his arms, and Jay lowered his hand at her waist. He figured that he had hurt her. Worried, Jay pulled back.

"I hurt you, damn it," he growled, annoyed with his forgetfulness. *'How the heck could I forget that Elle had been shot?'* Jay scolded himself.

"Don't worry, Jay," Ellen took his hand. "It was only a twinge, and for a few seconds."

"I'm sorry, Elle," Jay leaned his head and touched his forehead of hers. "I didn't mean to hurt you."

"I know, so don't fret so much," she whispered, and the tips of her fingers stroked his face.

"I just love you so much," Jay whispered as well, and grasping her wrist, he brought her fingers to his mouth and kissed every single one of them with care.

The man's words awoke the butterflies in Ellen's belly, and she shivered. Jay carefully drew her closer to him.

"I don't think I can live without you, sweetie," he said quietly. "I need you to be my wife. I want to bind you to me in any possible way, baby."

Ellen froze in his arms for a few seconds. Then, she pulled back to look straight into the man's eyes. His gaze flickered with intensity. Jay waited for her answer with trepidation.

When the minutes flew away, and the woman still didn't answer, he pulled back and laughed with self-derision.

"I see that you're thrilled," he noted. "Is it me or my whacky family that stops you from giving me an answer?" he asked and tried to stand up, but Ellen grasped his hand and held fast.

"Could you be patient at least once?" Ellen snapped at him. "It's not like I hear something like that every day," she said.

"All right, I'll wait," Jay agreed with relief. *'She didn't say no yet,'* he concluded.

Ellen shook her head and smiled at him. "You're so impatient sometimes. You have to give a girl the time to draw her breath," she shook her head once more. "Of course, I want you, Jay, and you don't have to bind me to you. I already belong to you, love," she whispered, blushing violently, and touched his mouth with her lips tenderly.

'Who had thought that I'd ever say something like that?' she wondered.

Jay caught her head in his hands and crushed his lips to hers at her words. He poured all his longing for Ellen into his kiss. He had just deepened his kiss when someone knocked on the door.

Furious, the man jumped off the couch and shouted, "I can't believe it. I can't believe it," he repeated.

He started with angry steps toward the door, but Ellen's voice stopped him. "Jay, calm down. We'll have enough time together. Don't say something you will regret later," she warned him.

"You didn't even say if you would be my wife," he noted. "And here they are, ruining everything," he gesticulated with annoyance.

"You're dense, man," Ellen waved her hand. "Of course, I'll be your wife."

Jay forgot about the door and came back to her with long strides. He merely pulled her up and crushed her to him. However, he paid attention not to squeeze where she was hurt this time. Jay lowered his head over hers and kissed her again.

The knocks on the door didn't stop. They became louder.

"Damn, I have to open that darn door," Jay drew back and gritted his teeth.

"It seems so," Ellen laughed merrily. "Go, Jay, what are you waiting for?" she asked.

"That they would go away," he confessed.

Ellen shook her head, "I don't think that wish of yours would come true."

"At least, you said yes," he replied, searching her eyes to make sure that he didn't misunderstand.

"Yes," she said. "I did say yes."

He nodded emphatically and asked, arching his eyebrows, "Christmas Day?"

She nodded and blushed. However, her eyes shone with expectation and happiness.

CHAPTER THIRTY

To arrange a wedding on Christmas Day didn't turn out to be a simple thing, but Marjorie prevailed. She was so happy for her younger son that she didn't take no from anyone, not from the pastor or the caterer.

Ellen and Jay chose a simple wedding at Jay's parents' house with all his family in attendance. Anna and Adam, Jay's grandparents, pleaded with Jay to invite Rebecca. Jay gave in after a while, but he warned his grandfather that he would throw the witch out if she did something to Ellen.

Ellen walked toward the makeshift altar wearing a white sheath that stopped just above her knees. Maggie, Jay's sister, had braided white flowers in the bride's hair. Marjorie had gifted Ellen with a sapphire heart, which hung from a delicate necklace. The sapphire matched the engagement ring that Jay had put on Ellen's finger a month before.

Jay watched Ellen coming toward him with intense light in his eyes. Matt put his hand on the man's shoulder and squeezed. "I know how you feel, man. I was in your shoes. Just think that no one would come between the two of you from now on," he whispered to his brother.

Jay nodded, but his eyes glanced at Rebecca right away. The old woman watched everything with narrowed eyes, and her mouth was a thin line. '*She's hatching something,*' the man thought, and his heart squeezed.

Ellen noticed the change in his mood at once, and she shifted her eyes toward Rebecca, too. *'Just try to ruin his day,'* she warned the woman mentally. 'I'll have your head.'

Everyone laughed when the bride reached the groom. Jay pulled her to him with a possessive gesture and kissed her soundly.

The old pastor cleared his throat and warned him, "That comes at the end, young man. You need a little patience."

"Told you so," Ellen said to Jay, with laughter in her eyes.

"You imp," he whispered and tweaked her nose.

"Can we start this wedding, folks?" the pastor inquired, gazing at his watch. His wife had invited people over for Christmas, and he had to get back home in less than an hour.

"Of course," Jay waved his hand as if he had done a favour to the old man.

The pastor pierced him with his eyes. "You've always been an irreverent young man," he shook his head.

The ceremony began amid chuckles from everyone seated in Marjorie's living room except Rebecca. The pastor droned on and on about the sanctity of marriage, and Jay crossed his eyes. He wanted to get to where the pastor declared that they were husband and wife and be done with all the ceremony.

The pastor made the mistake of asking if anyone knew of any reason the two young people shouldn't marry. Rebecca grasped her chance with both her hands and said in a challenging tone of voice, "Of course, I do. They don't love each other. This is only a masquerade. This wedding shouldn't take place."

Jay saw red before his eyes and turned to get to her. He didn't know what he would do when he reached the old woman, but the darkness of his features scared Ellen. She grabbed his hand with all her might.

"No, Jay. She isn't worth it," she shouted to the man because he didn't seem to see anything else but the old woman's face.

Ellen's fear was evident on her features, and Matt grasped his brother's arm as well.

"Jay, stop it. She isn't worth it. You're scaring Ellen," Matt said in a calm tone of voice.

"Did you hear what the witch said?" Jay shouted.

"I did, but no one believes her. Isn't it so?" Matt turned to the pastor and levelled his hard look on the man.

The pastor swallowed hard and nodded. "Of course, we can continue with the wedding," the old man observed. *'Even if it is true, it's not the first couple that gets married without love after all,'* he reflected.

Ellen squeezed Jay's hand again, and her gaze pleaded with him. Jay turned his eyes at her and brought her hand to his mouth.

"Let's make you mine, sweetie," he smiled at her, deciding not to pay any attention to his great-grandmother.

The pastor breathed with relief. He had come there for a wedding, not a murder.

When the ceremony ended and Ellen had finally become his wife, Jay hugged her with all his might and kissed her passionately for everyone to see.

"Finally, you'll sleep in my bed tonight," he shouted, completely forgetting about the others, and Ellen turned scarlet.

"Jay," she slapped his arm. "Have you lost your mind to shout something like that?" she wondered.

People were laughing around them, and even the severe pastor smiled with a shake of his head. *'Huh, they don't love each other,'* he scoffed. *'Rebecca has lost her mind,'* he decided.

"Sorry, sweetie," Jay apologized. "I'm just happy," he brushed his lips over her knuckles.

Then, he squeezed her hand again and pulled her toward the family. When his eyes fell on Rebecca, he decreed in a stern tone of voice, "You're out of here. Right this moment."

Afterward, he led his new wife to his parents. Marjory hugged Ellen with tears of joy in her eyes. "You've made my boy so happy," she whispered. "I can't thank you enough."

"I ALWAYS LOVED CHRISTMAS," Jay whispered to Ellen, holding her in his arms. They were lying under the tree they had decorated together and gazing into each other's eyes. "I loved most the Christmas presents I found under the tree in the morning," he admitted with a chuckle. "But I've never known that one day, I'll find the best gift ever under my own Christmas tree," he reckoned in a sober tone of voice.

The man raised Ellen's hand and gazed at the ring he had put on her finger a few hours earlier and said quietly, "Mine. You belong only to me now."

AUTHOR'S BIO

ROWENA DAWN writes romance, reads thrillers, and watches comedies. She likes walking through the woods but insanely loves the sea. She has a love-hate relationship with her writing and drives her dog crazy whenever she doesn't stop writing to take him out.

OTHER BOOKS BY ROWENA DAWN

LEAP OF FAITH
Double-Edged – Book One in The Perfect Halves Series
Eyes in the Dark – Book Two in The Perfect Halves Series
Pulled In – Book Three in The Perfect Halves Series
Becka's Awakening – Book One in The Winstons Series
Matt's Dilemma – Book Two in The Winstons Series
Jay's Salvation – Book Three in The Winstons Series
Catching Lily – Live Wire – Book Four in The Perfect Halves Series & The Winstons Series
Ariel's Redemption – Book Five in The Winstons Series
Forthcoming:
Alex's Wake Up Call - Book Six in The Winstons Series

Did you love *Jay's Salvation*? Then you should read *Catching Lily - Live Wire*[1] by Rowena Dawn!

Lily has almost given up on her happily ever after. Mark is just on the run and hopes to keep his hide intact.

A chance encounter makes Lily hope again, and Mark find his stopping point.

Lily comes from a family of witches, and she has got a curse over her head. The Winston family is large, full of wonders, happiness, but also bitterness.

1. https://books2read.com/u/47EMeN

2. https://books2read.com/u/47EMeN

Mark is her chance to get involved with a man who resembles no one she has ever known. He is a strong man, full of secrets, and almost cold-hearted. Mark seizes his chance with Lily, but two questions remain to be answered. Will his past chase her away? Will her family secret come between the two of them?

Lily and Mark bring together the characters of two romance series, infusing their lives both with suspense and paranormal.

About the Publisher

It is based in Toronto and brings to public various books: poems, novels, short-stories, children's books, language study books and non-fiction. It publishes the literary review: Scarlet Leaf Review: www.scarletleafreview.com

Our mission is to help emerging authors and poets to make their works known to the public.

Contact email address: scarletleafpublishinghouse@gmail.com

www.ingramcontent.com/pod-product-compliance
Lightning Source LLC
Chambersburg PA
CBHW071250250626
47163CB00002B/412